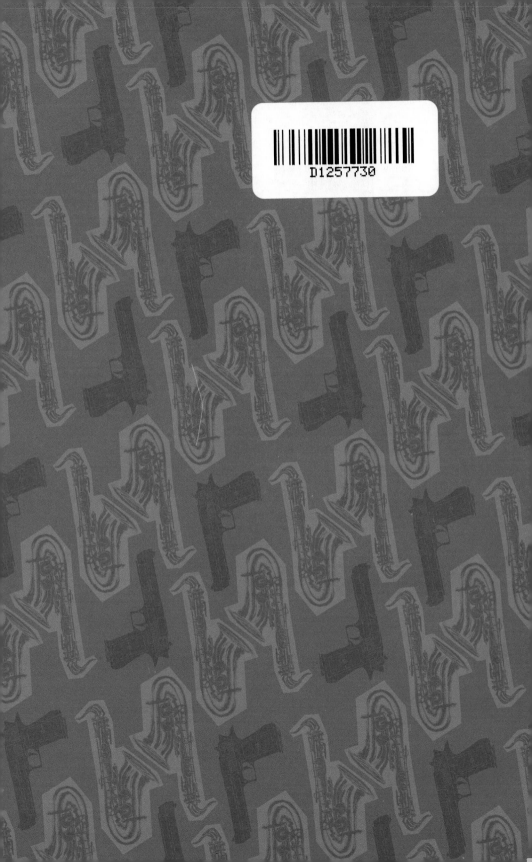

LAST FAIR DEAL
GONE DOWN

12-GAUGE COMICS, LLC

Keven Gardner, President
Doug Wagner, Managing Editor
Brian Stelfreeze, Art Director
Eben Matthews, Director of New Media
Jason Pearson, Creative Consultant
Cully Hamner, Creative Consultant

www.12gaugecomics.com

/12gaugecomics

@12gaugecomics

/12gaugecomics

12gaugecomics.tumblrcom

Book Design by Eben Matthews

ISBN: 978-0-9836937-1-0

**NICK TRAVERS VOLUME 1: LAST FAIR DEAL GONE DOWN.
MAY 2016. FIRST PRINTING.**
Last Fair Deal Gone Down is © 2016 Ace Atkins.
12-Gauge Comics, LLC authorized user. All Rights Reserved.

LAST FAIR DEAL GONE DOWN

A NICK TRAVERS GRAPHIC NOVEL

Story **ACE ATKINS**

Art & Letters **MARCO FINNEGAN**

Cover **CHRIS BRUNNER**

Editor **KEVEN GARDNER**

12-GAUGE

INTRODUCTION

The journey for this story you hold in your hands has been long and winding to say the least. I wrote *Last Fair Deal Gone Down* twenty years ago in a studio apartment in Tampa, Florida, where I was working as a newspaper reporter. After struggling for several years with a novel that would never be published – nor should it ever – *Last Fair Deal* was the first story I'd written that I felt really worked and was solid. Reading my first abandoned manuscript, my friend, the novelist Tim Green, advised me to stick with what really worked: crime, the blues, and New Orleans. I distilled this all into this short story, and from it sprang four Nick Travers novels. But *Last Fair Deal* was the last to be published. The reason: there isn't much of a market for short fiction, let alone a story the length of a short novella.

For more than a decade, the story was lost, relegated to an old hard drive and pretty much forgotten except for what it contributed to my inspiration for the Nick Travers novels. If not for my late friend David Thompson, it would've remained there, possibly vanishing forever. In 2007, David, who had started a small press in Houston, wanted to publish a new edition of *Crossroad Blues*, the first Nick Travers novel. With the edition, he asked me if I had any new or unpublished material to accompany the book. When I mentioned *Last Fair Deal* being the springboard for all the Nick Travers stories, he leapt at the chance to publish it for the first time. The next year, the short story would be a finalist for the Edgar Allan Poe Awards. It was a happy time for Nick Travers. David planned to bring back all four novels, and we talked about new books that never happened. Months later, David, only 37, died of an undetected heart condition. This volume is dedicated to his memory.

That would be pretty much the end of this story, and possibly the epitaph to Nick Travers himself, had it not been for a southern California ink-slinger named Marco Finnegan. Marco reached out to me through Twitter about my continuation of the Robert B. Parker *Spenser* novels. For months, Marco sent some incredible sketches of Spenser, and soon that crossed over into drawings of my own creations. Soon he asked: "Any ideas for a graphic novel?"

We played around with several ideas until we circled back to Nick. Within days, Marco drew some absolutely mind-blowing sketches – bringing to life the words I'd put on page all those years ago. Once we had a plan, we discussed publishers who were into hardboiled Southern stories and centered on the only company for the job – 12 Gauge Comics.

Now, here is where the story gets a little weird. Nick Travers has roots in my time as an undergrad at Auburn University in Alabama. 12 Gauge is based in Alabama, and its publisher, Keven Gardner, is not only an Auburn grad but attended college at the same time as me. We figured we probably passed each other in the halls as I was just starting to scribble out ideas for Nick in spiral notebooks.

It took a southern California artist to bring together two Alabama natives and Auburn alums to publish Deep South Noir. Once Marco received the green light from Keven, the story grew and took shape in ways beyond my wildest expectations. He did what I thought impossible – he brought Nick Travers back to life.

As you'll note on this comic, we call it Volume #1, and that's exactly what's intended. Marco is already plotting out and drawing images from *Crossroad Blues*, and from there, who knows what's next. Nick is a character who not only refuses to die but has been afforded the good fortune of many talented people who keep on bringing him out of retirement. It's a rare thing to work with an artist like Marco. Not only are his drawings incredible, but he has an uncanny ability to understand what's intended between my lines. A friend to me and Nick Travers, he understands the motivations and the mindset of this Southern hero.

Just recently, I returned to New Orleans, walking in footsteps of Nick Travers' world. I crossed Royal and into Jackson Square, realizing so much had changed in the city, but so much stayed the same. Once again, I believe that somewhere out there, Nick walks those same mean streets.

- Ace Atkins
- Oxford, Mississippi 2016

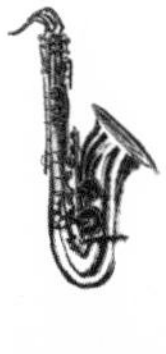

For my wife, Lisa, without whom
this would not have been possible.
-**Marco**

For David Thompson.
-Ace

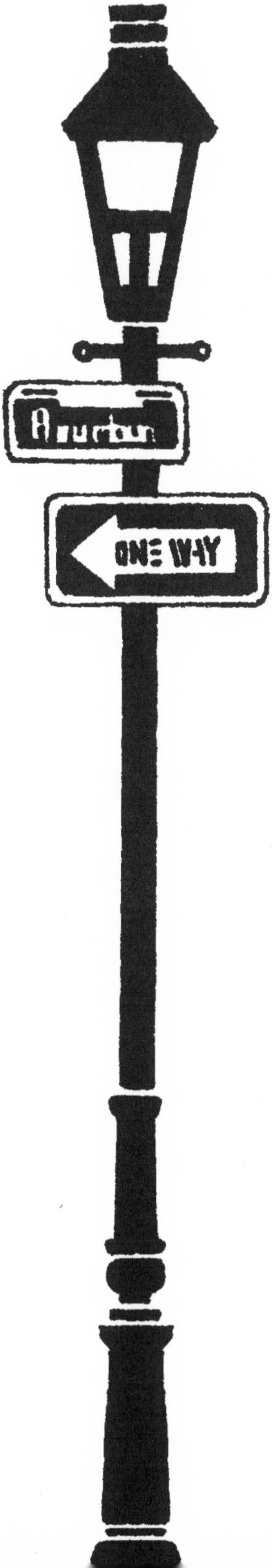
ONE WAY

CHAPTER ONE

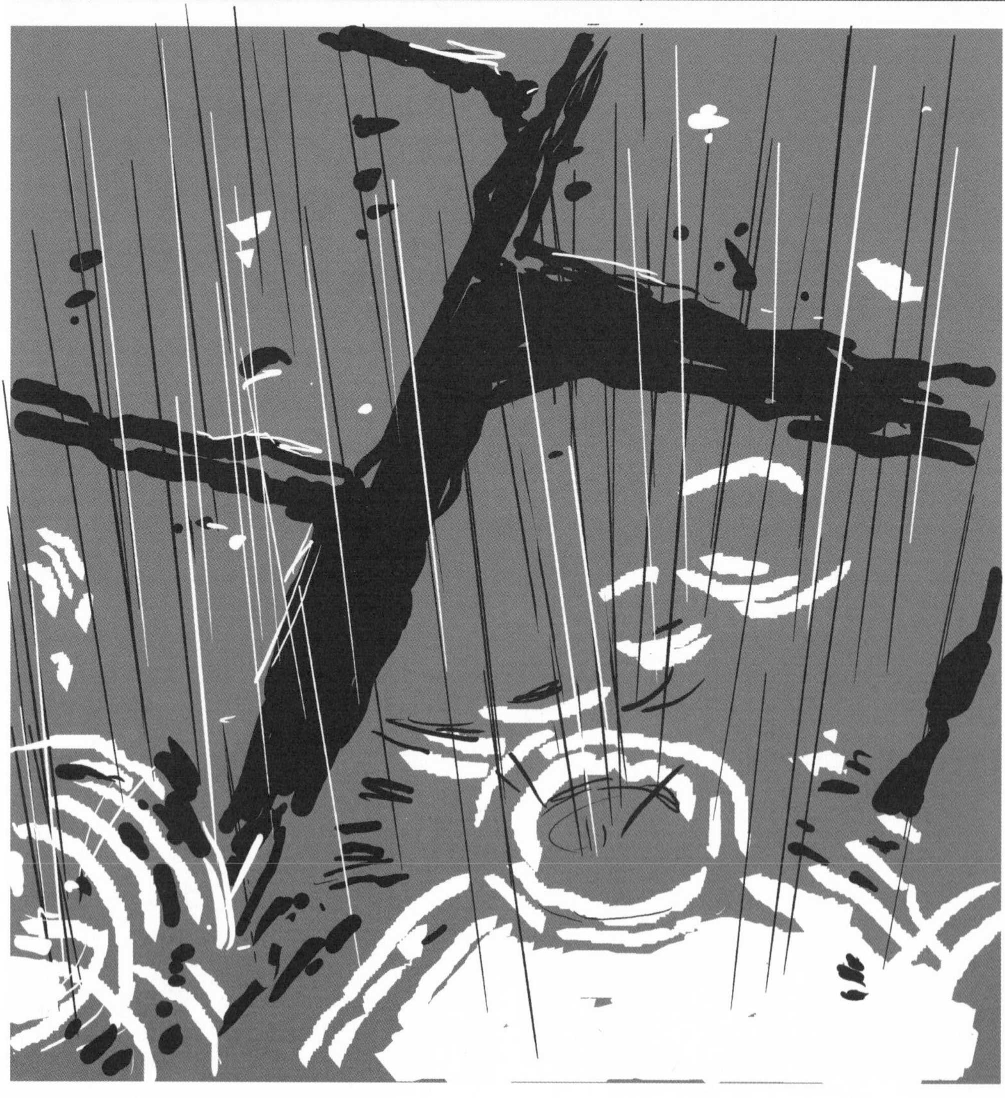

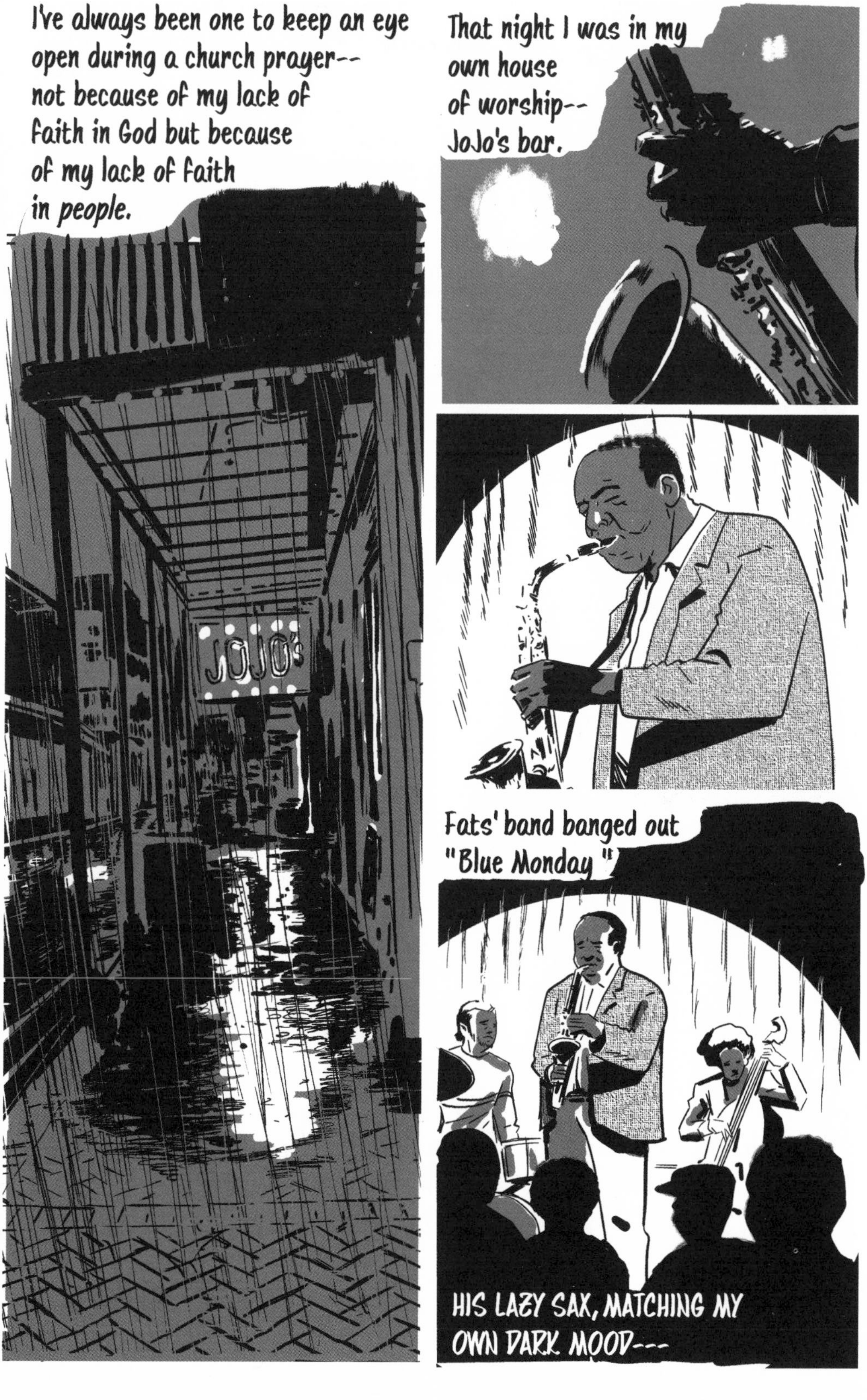
I've always been one to keep an eye open during a church prayer--not because of my lack of faith in God but because of my lack of faith in *people.*
JOJO'S
That night I was in my own house of worship--JoJo's bar.
Fats' band banged out "Blue Monday"
HIS LAZY SAX, MATCHING MY OWN DARK MOOD---

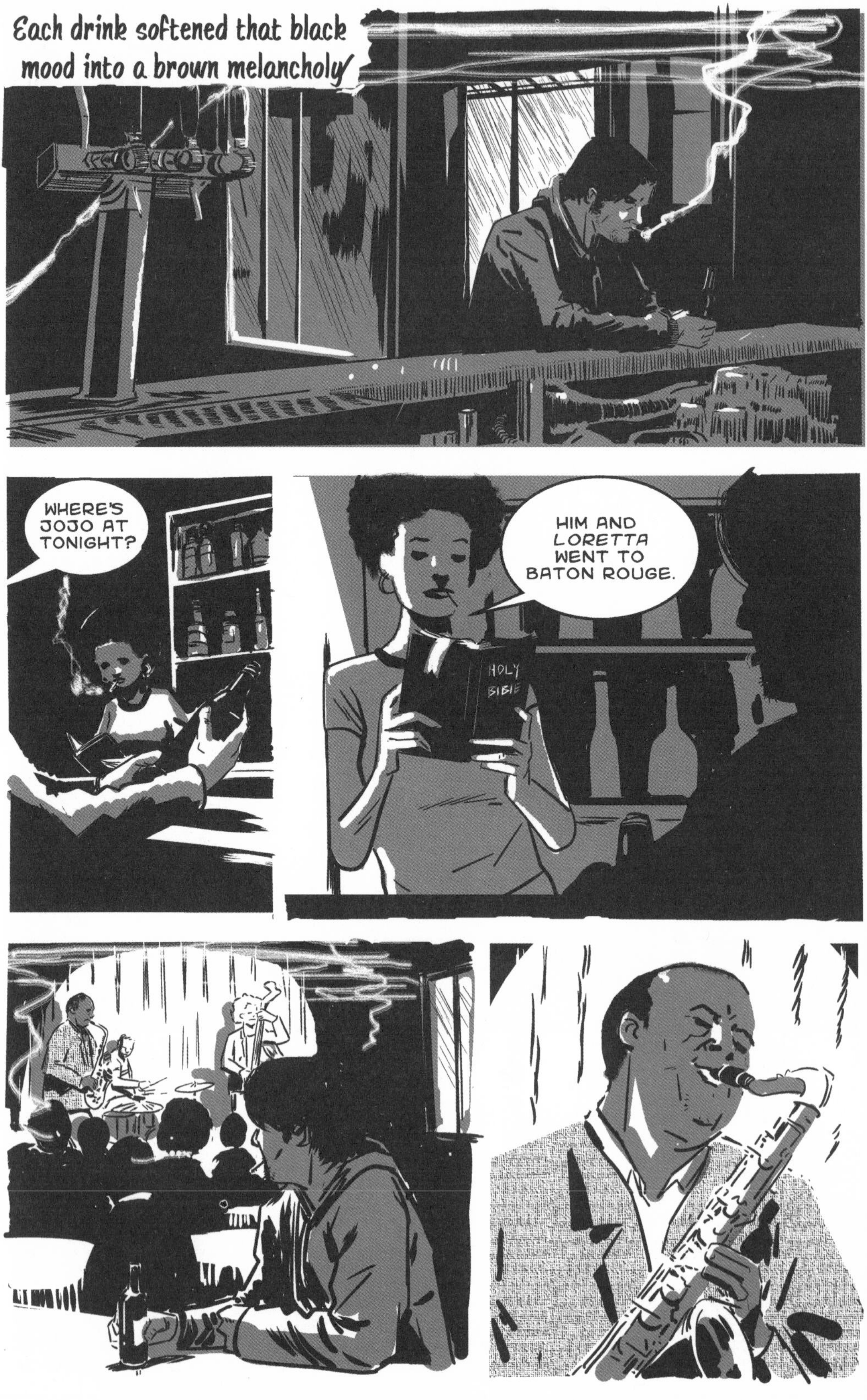
Each drink softened that black mood into a brown melancholy.
WHERE'S JOJO AT TONIGHT?
HIM AND LORETTA WENT TO BATON ROUGE.
HOLY BIBLE

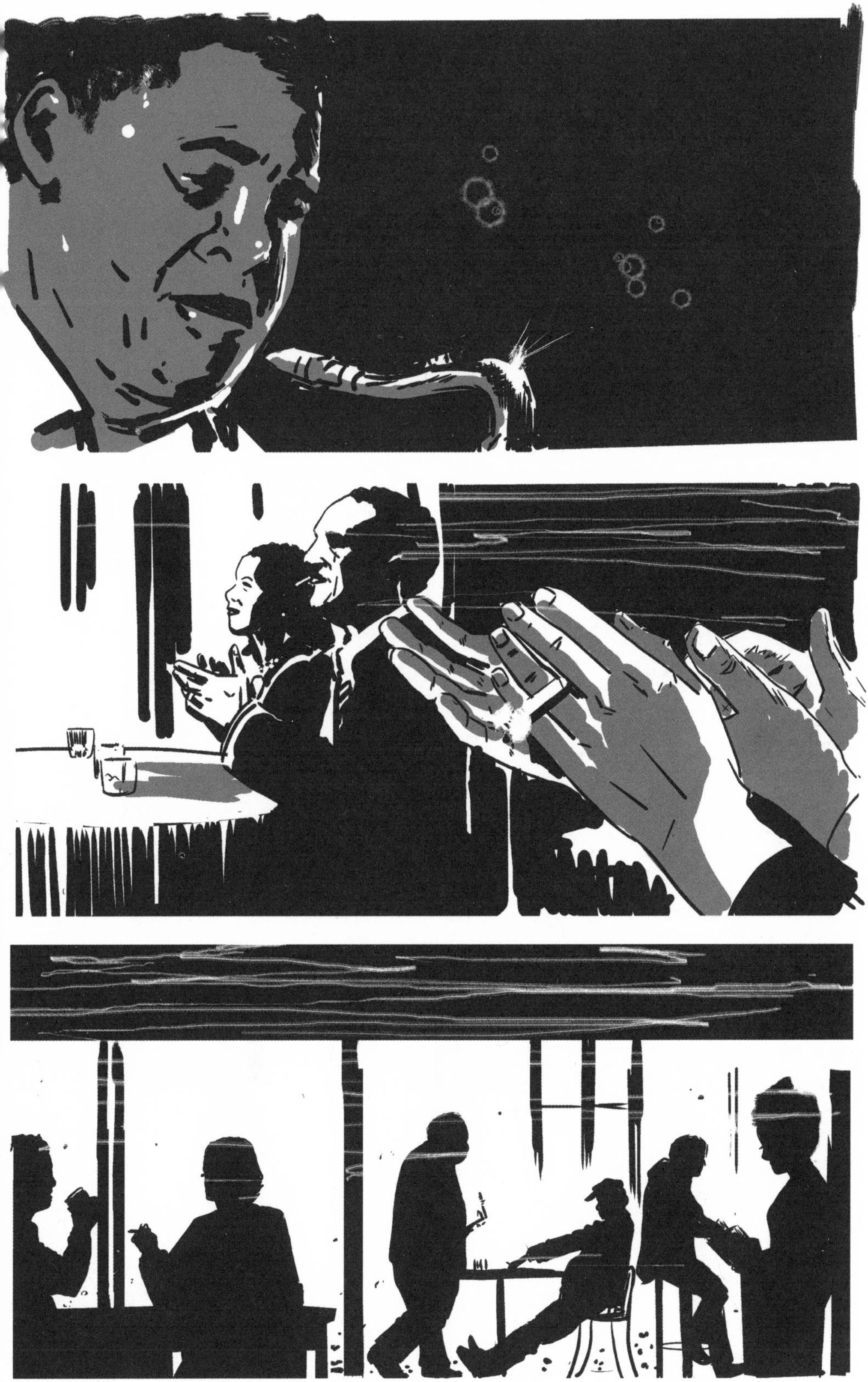

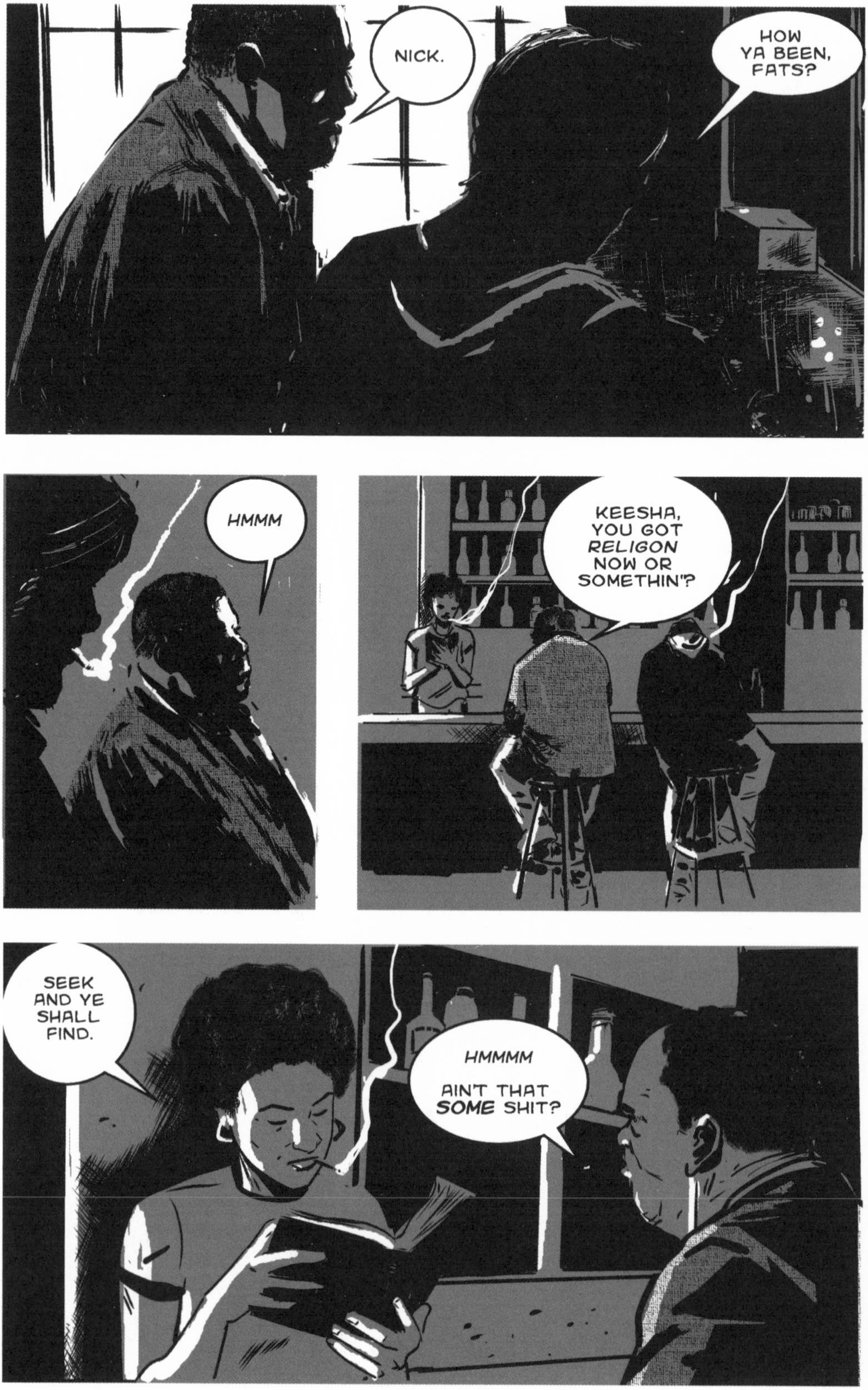
NICK.
HOW YA BEEN, FATS?
HMMM
KEESHA, YOU GOT *RELIGON* NOW OR SOMETHIN'?
SEEK AND YE SHALL FIND.
HMMMM
AIN'T THAT **SOME** SHIT?

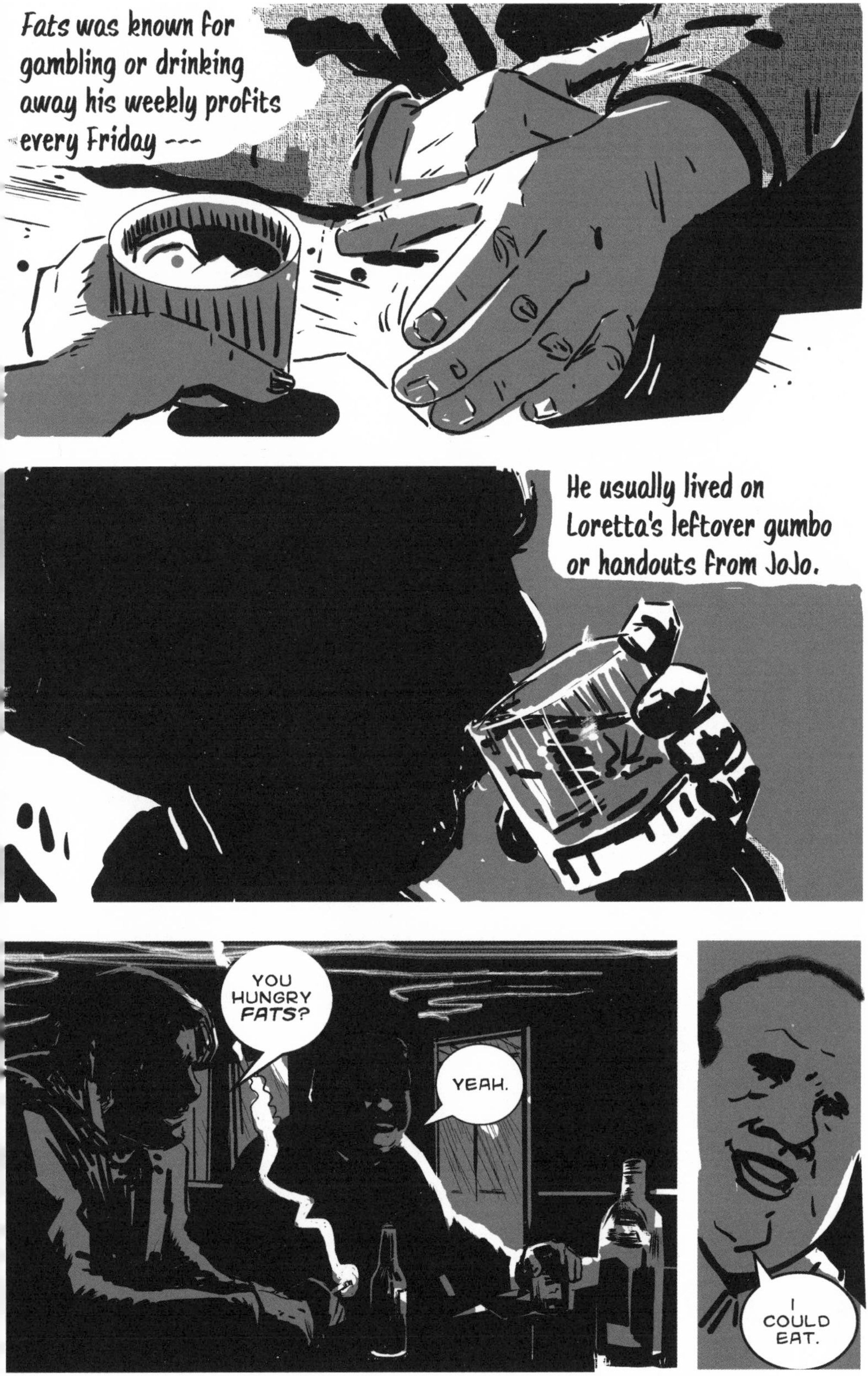
Fats was known for gambling or drinking away his weekly profits every Friday ---
He usually lived on Loretta's leftover gumbo or handouts from JoJo.
YOU HUNGRY FATS?
YEAH.
I COULD EAT.

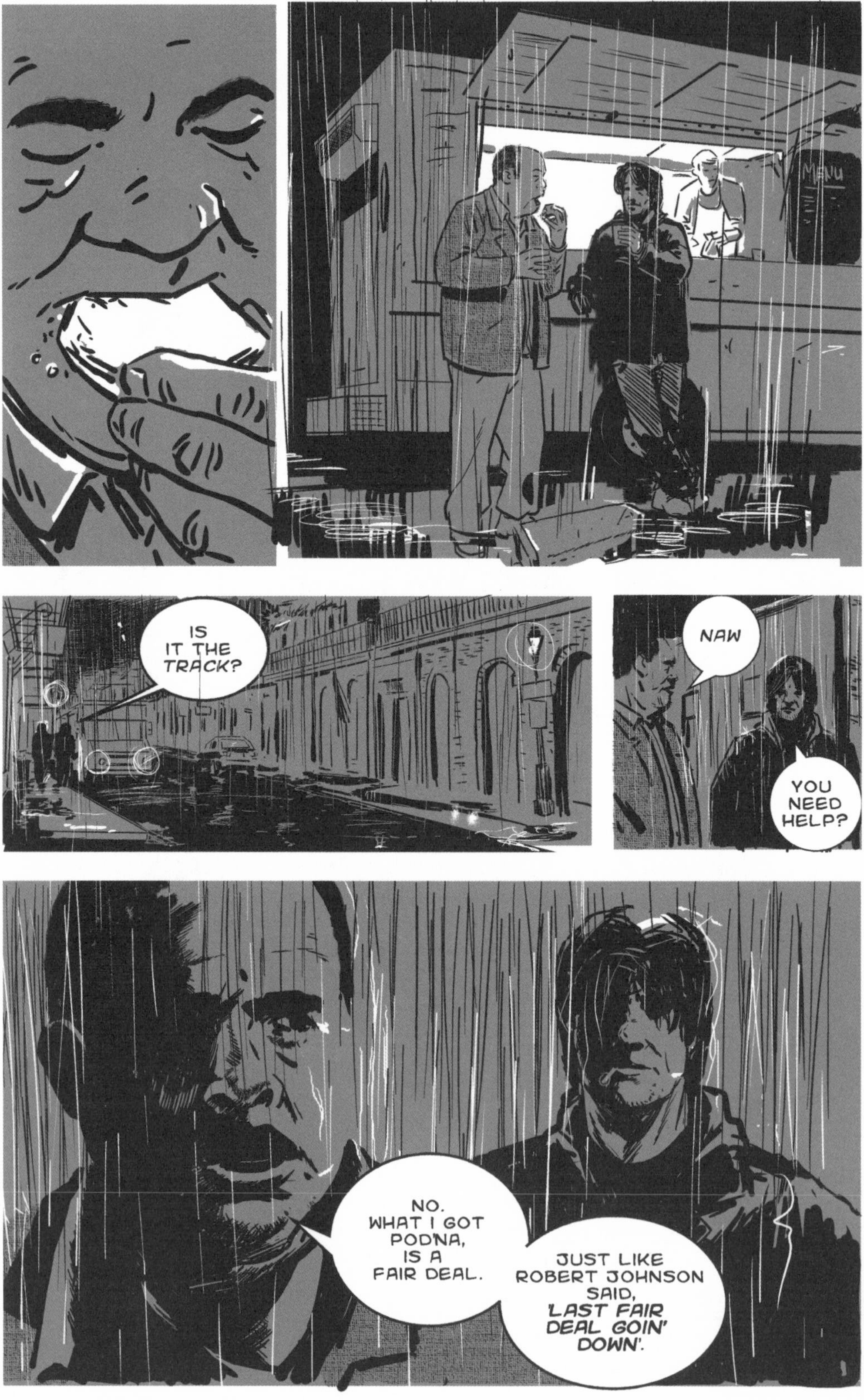
IS IT THE TRACK?
NAW
YOU NEED HELP?
NO. WHAT I GOT POD'NA, IS A FAIR DEAL.
JUST LIKE ROBERT JOHNSON SAID, 'LAST FAIR DEAL GOIN' DOWN'.
MENU

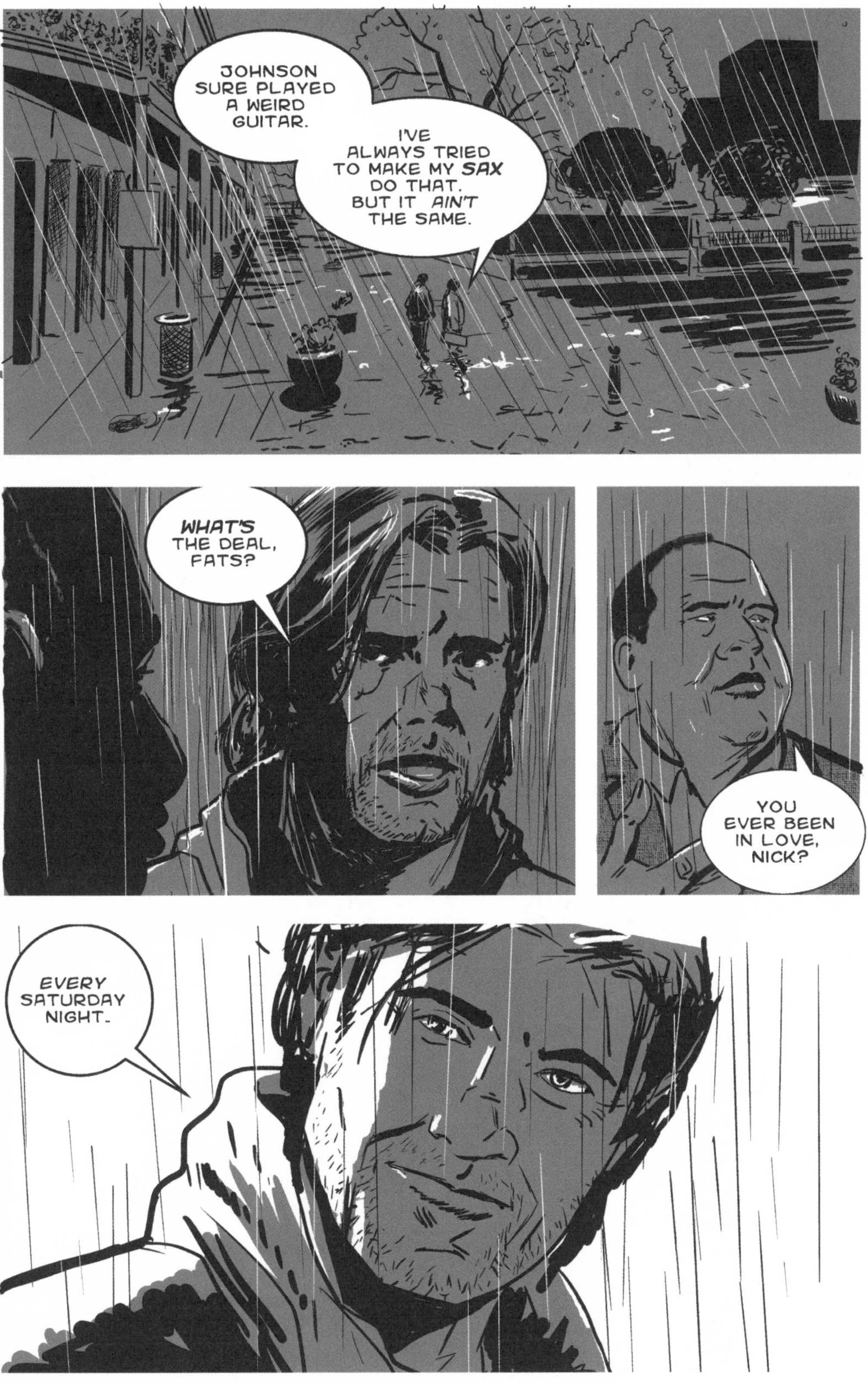
JOHNSON SURE PLAYED A WEIRD GUITAR.
I'VE ALWAYS TRIED TO MAKE MY *SAX* DO THAT. BUT IT *AIN'T* THE SAME.
WHAT'S THE DEAL, FATS?
YOU EVER BEEN IN LOVE, NICK?
EVERY SATURDAY NIGHT.

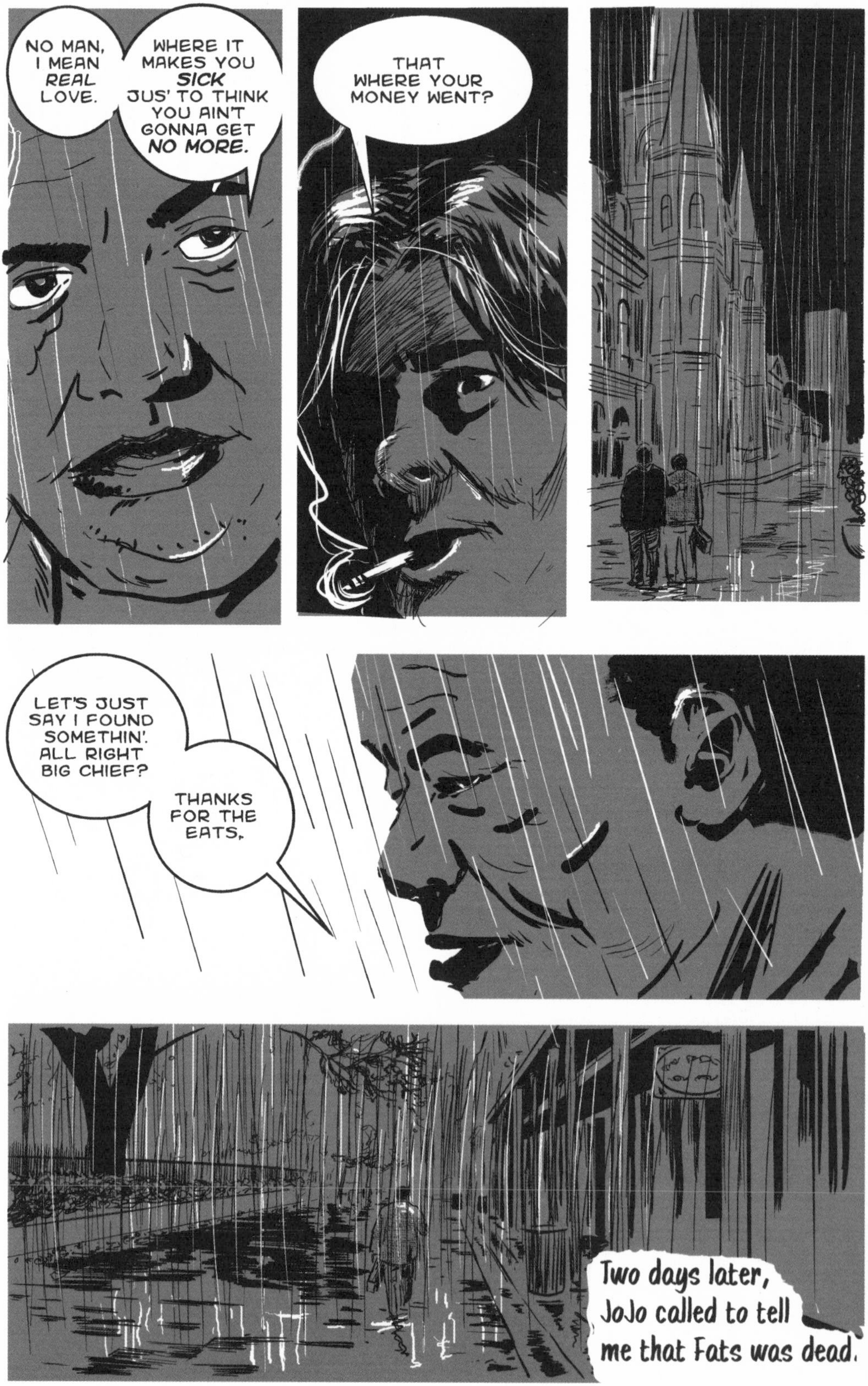
NO MAN, I MEAN REAL LOVE.
WHERE IT MAKES YOU SICK JUS' TO THINK YOU AIN'T GONNA GET NO MORE.
THAT WHERE YOUR MONEY WENT?
LET'S JUST SAY I FOUND SOMETHIN'. ALL RIGHT BIG CHIEF?
THANKS FOR THE EATS.
Two days later, JoJo called to tell me that Fats was dead.

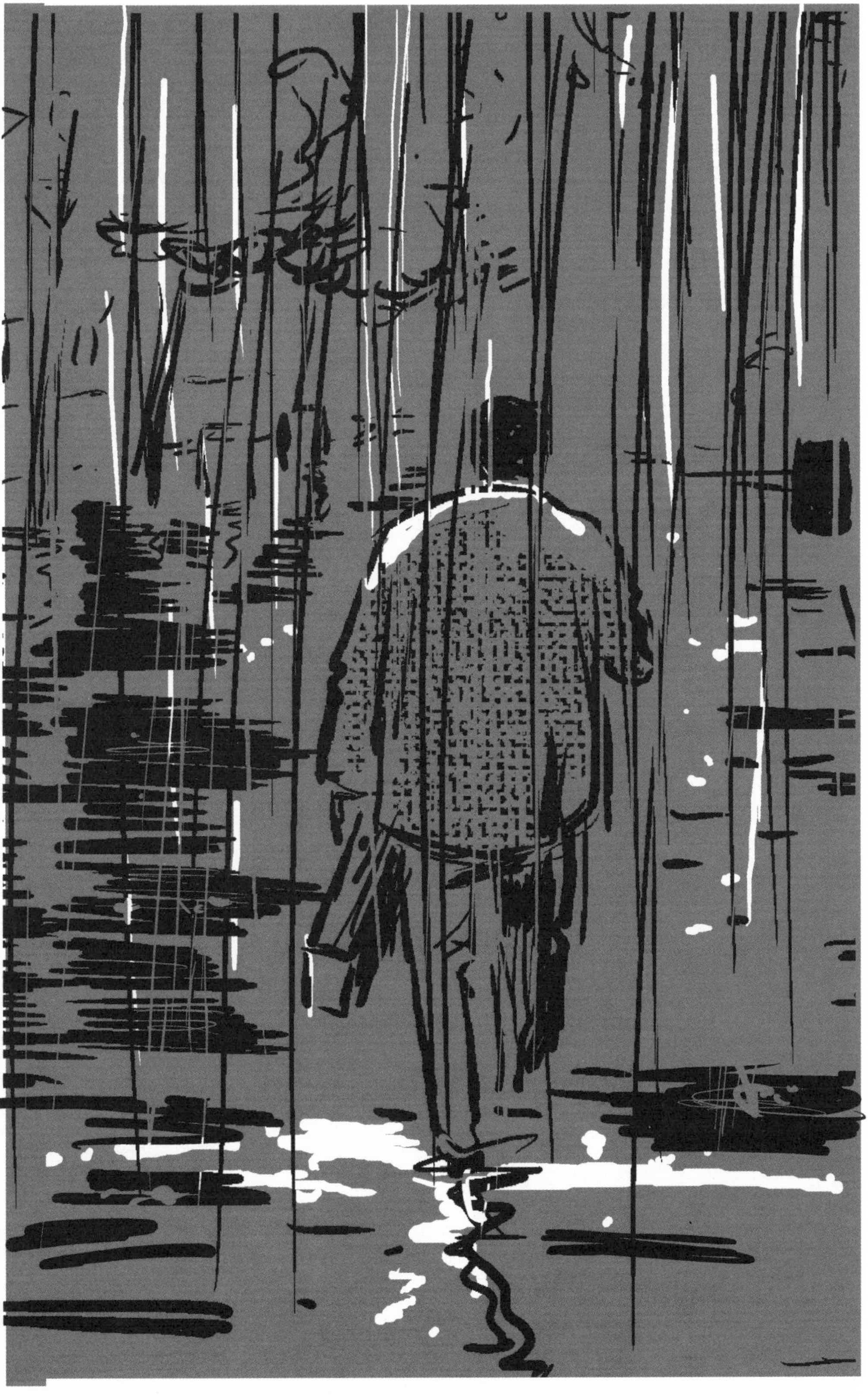

CHAPTER TWO

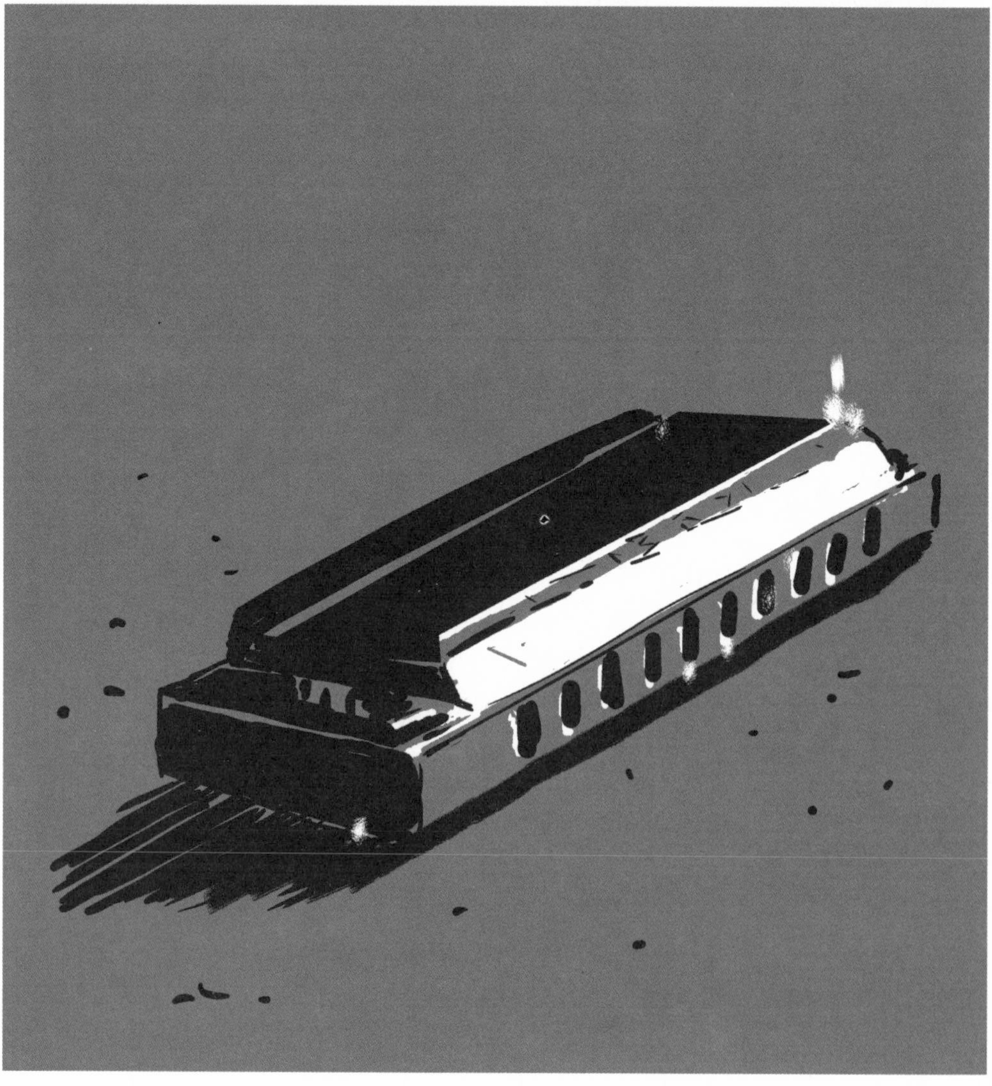

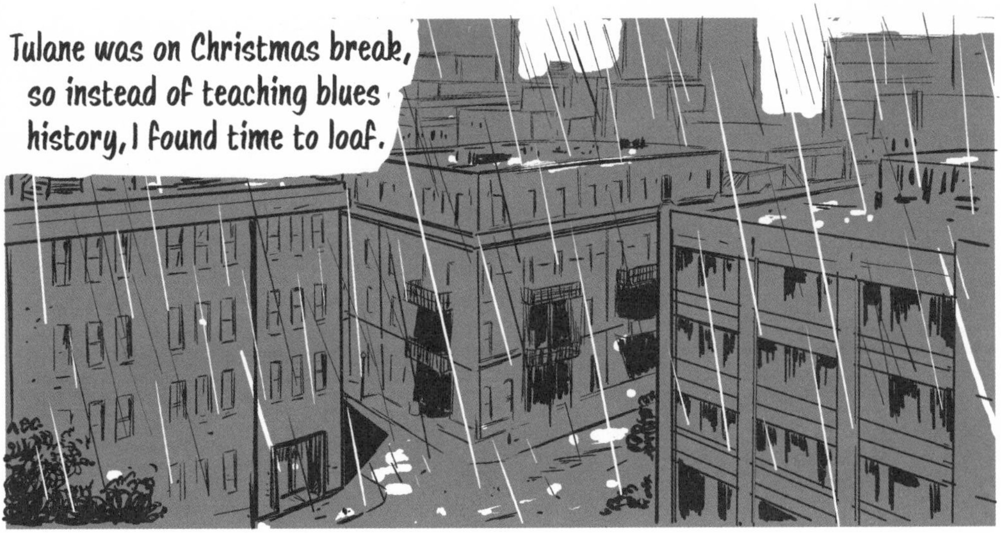
Tulane was on Christmas break, so instead of teaching blues history, I found time to loaf.

I was practicing some of Little Walter's harp licks on my Hohner Special 20 when my door buzzed.

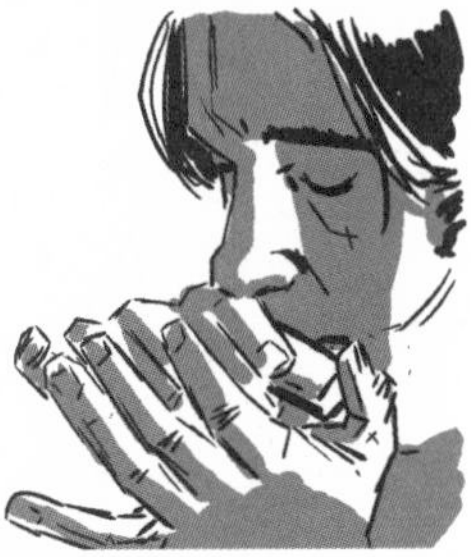

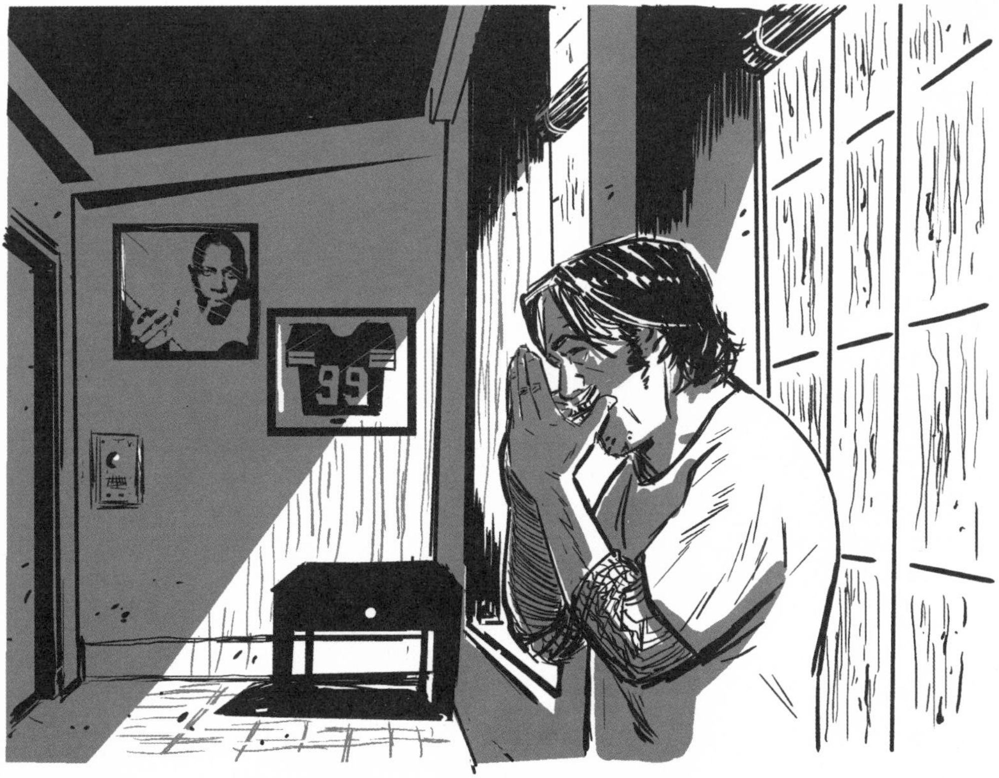

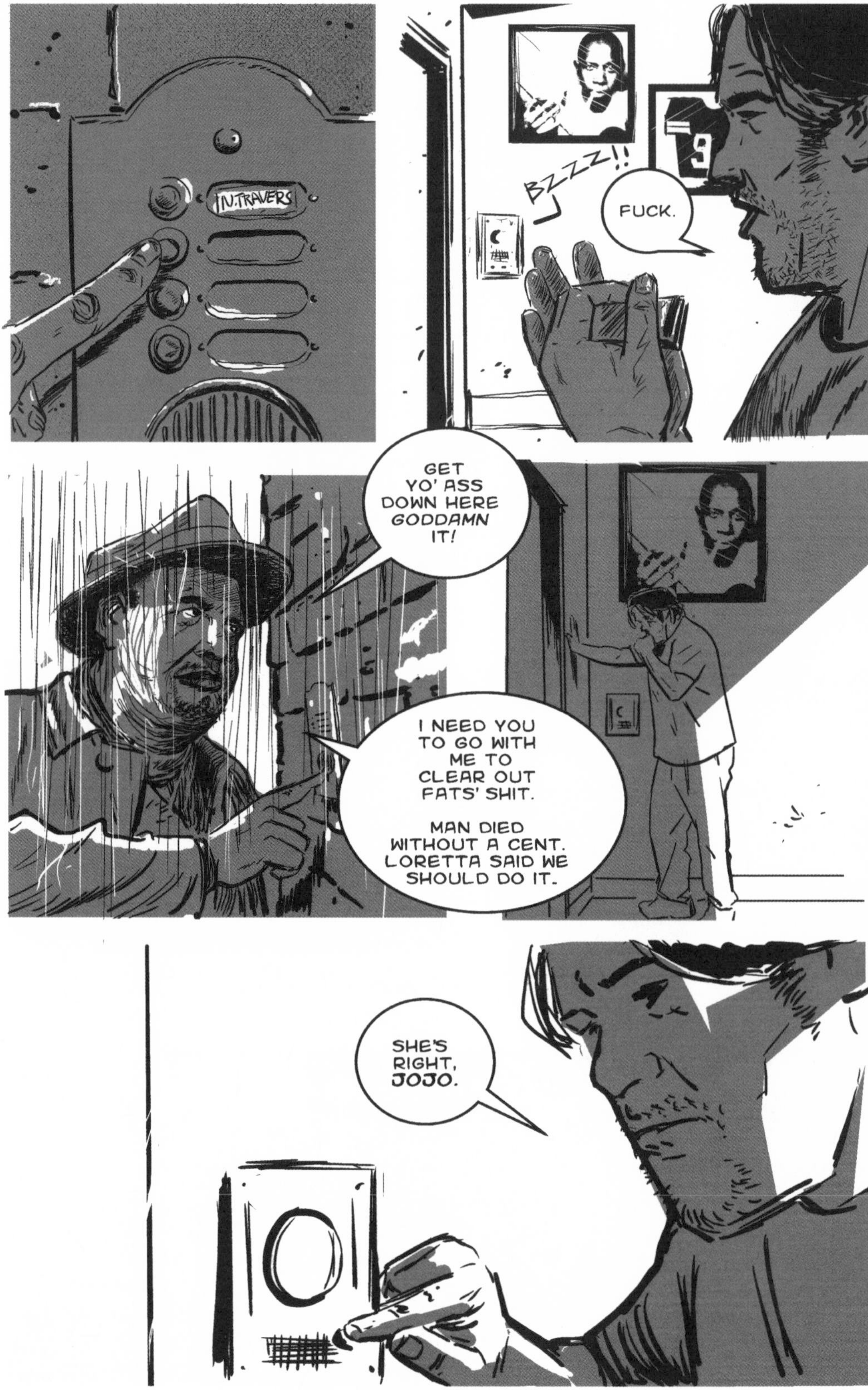
N.TRAVERS
BZZZZ!!
FUCK.
GET YO' ASS DOWN HERE GODDAMN IT!
I NEED YOU TO GO WITH ME TO CLEAR OUT FATS' SHIT.
MAN DIED WITHOUT A CENT. LORETTA SAID WE SHOULD DO IT.
SHE'S RIGHT, JOJO.

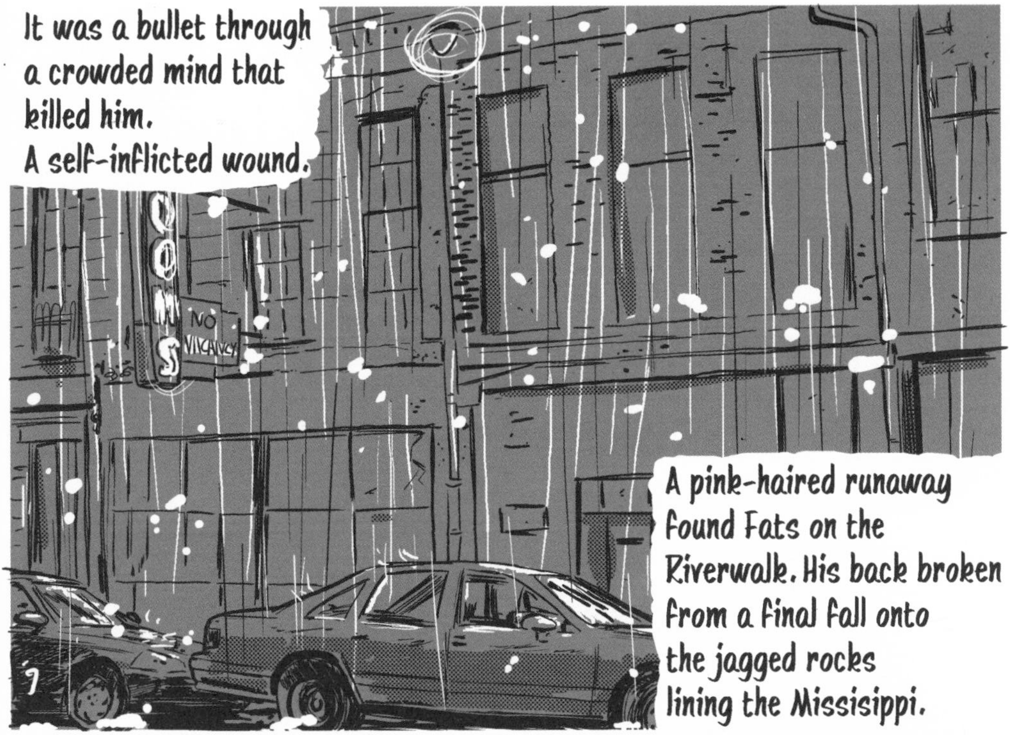
It was a bullet through a crowded mind that killed him.
A self-inflicted wound.
A pink-haired runaway found Fats on the Riverwalk. His back broken from a final fall onto the jagged rocks lining the Missisippi.

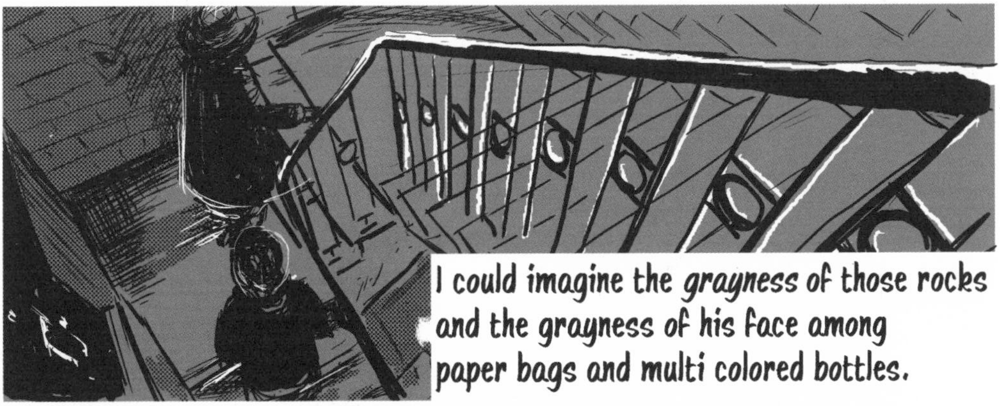
I could imagine the *grayness* of those rocks and the grayness of his face among paper bags and multi colored bottles.

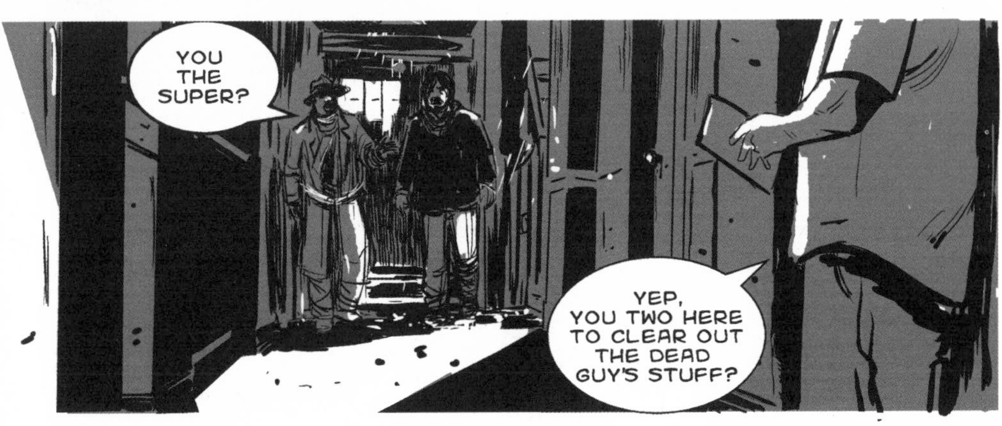
YOU THE SUPER?
YEP, YOU TWO HERE TO CLEAR OUT THE DEAD GUY'S STUFF?

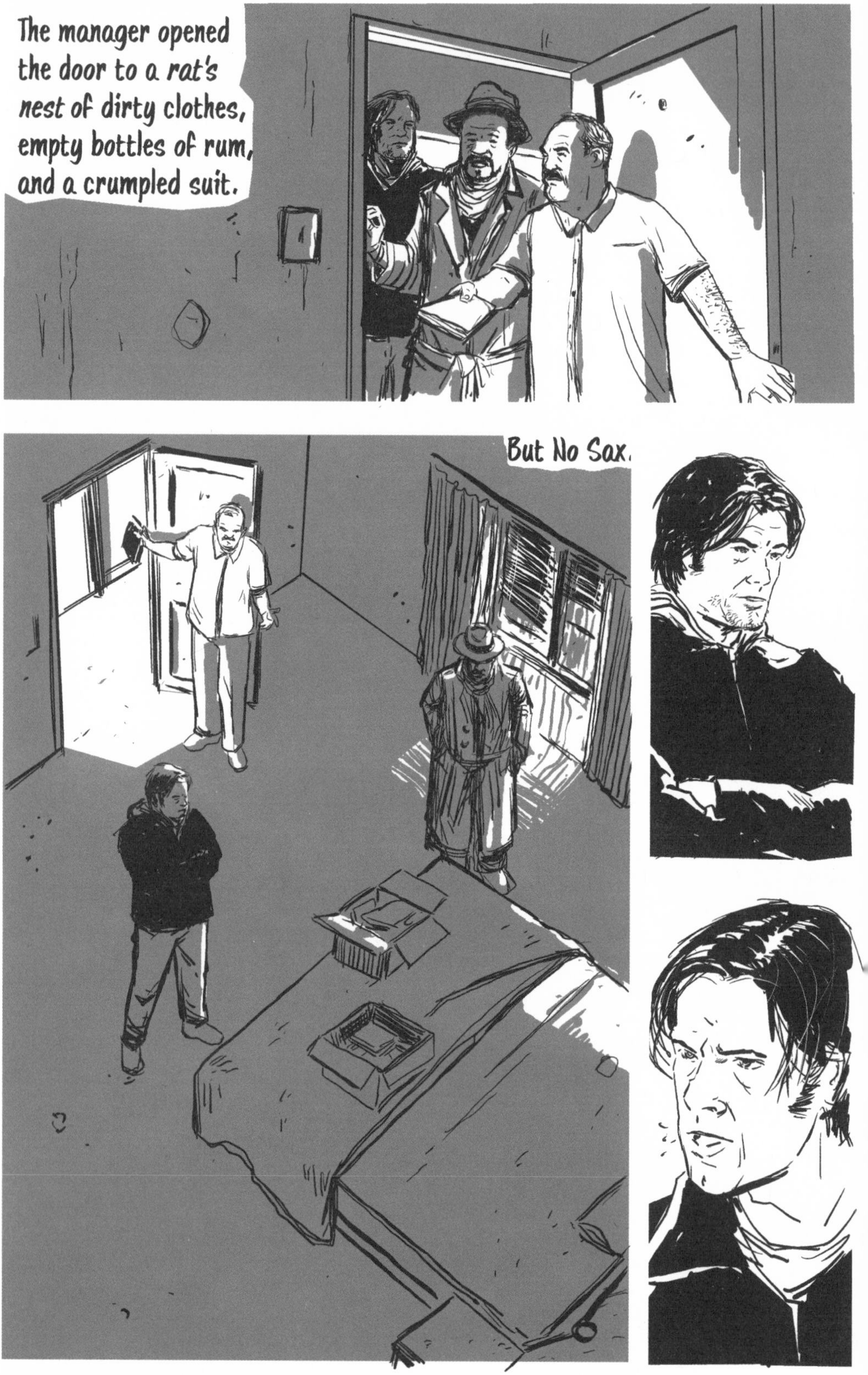
The manager opened the door to a rat's nest of dirty clothes, empty bottles of rum, and a crumpled suit.
But No Sax.

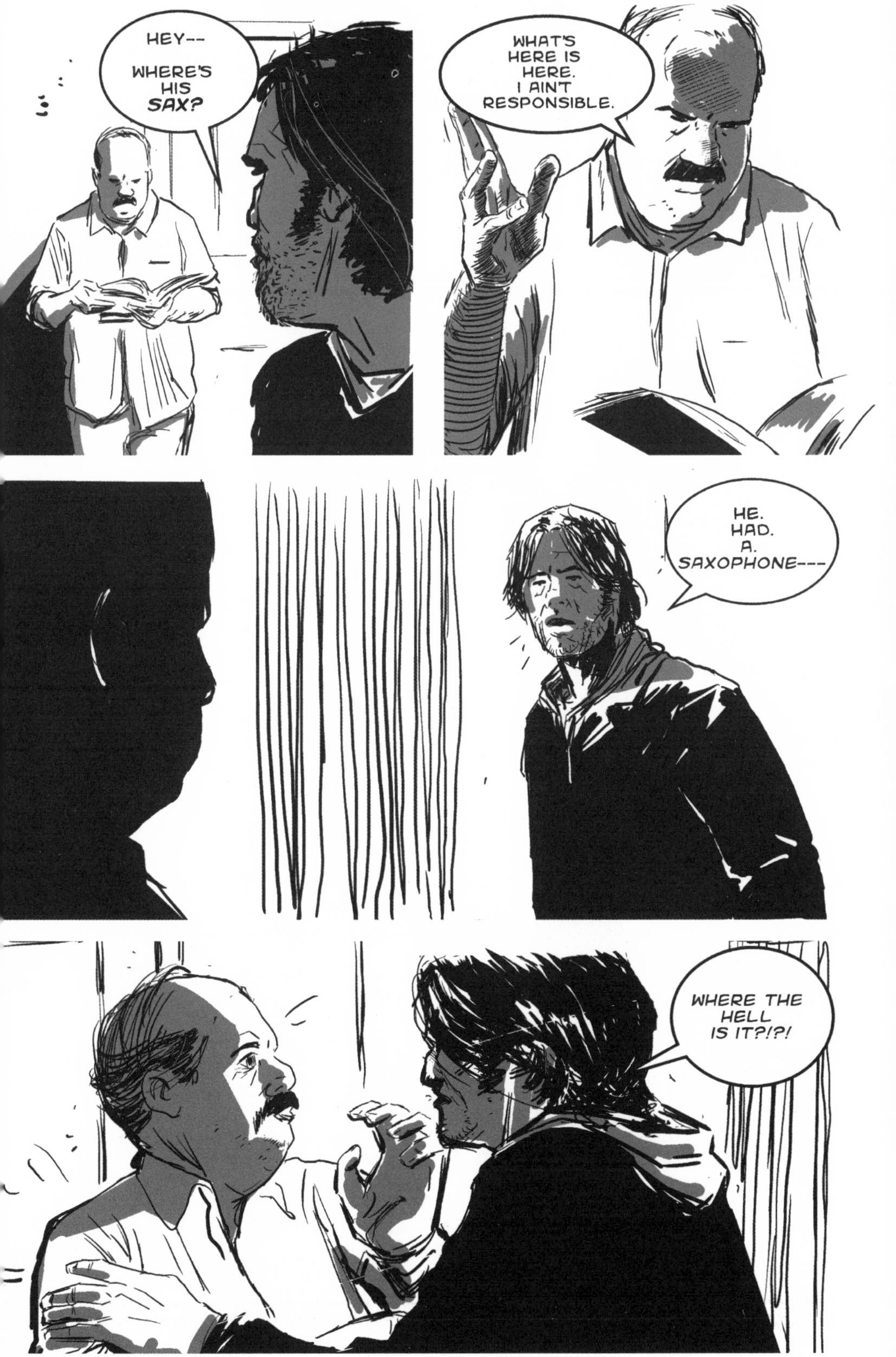
HEY--
WHERE'S HIS *SAX?*
WHAT'S HERE IS HERE. I AIN'T RESPONSIBLE.
HE. HAD. A. SAXOPHONE---
WHERE THE HELL IS IT?!?!

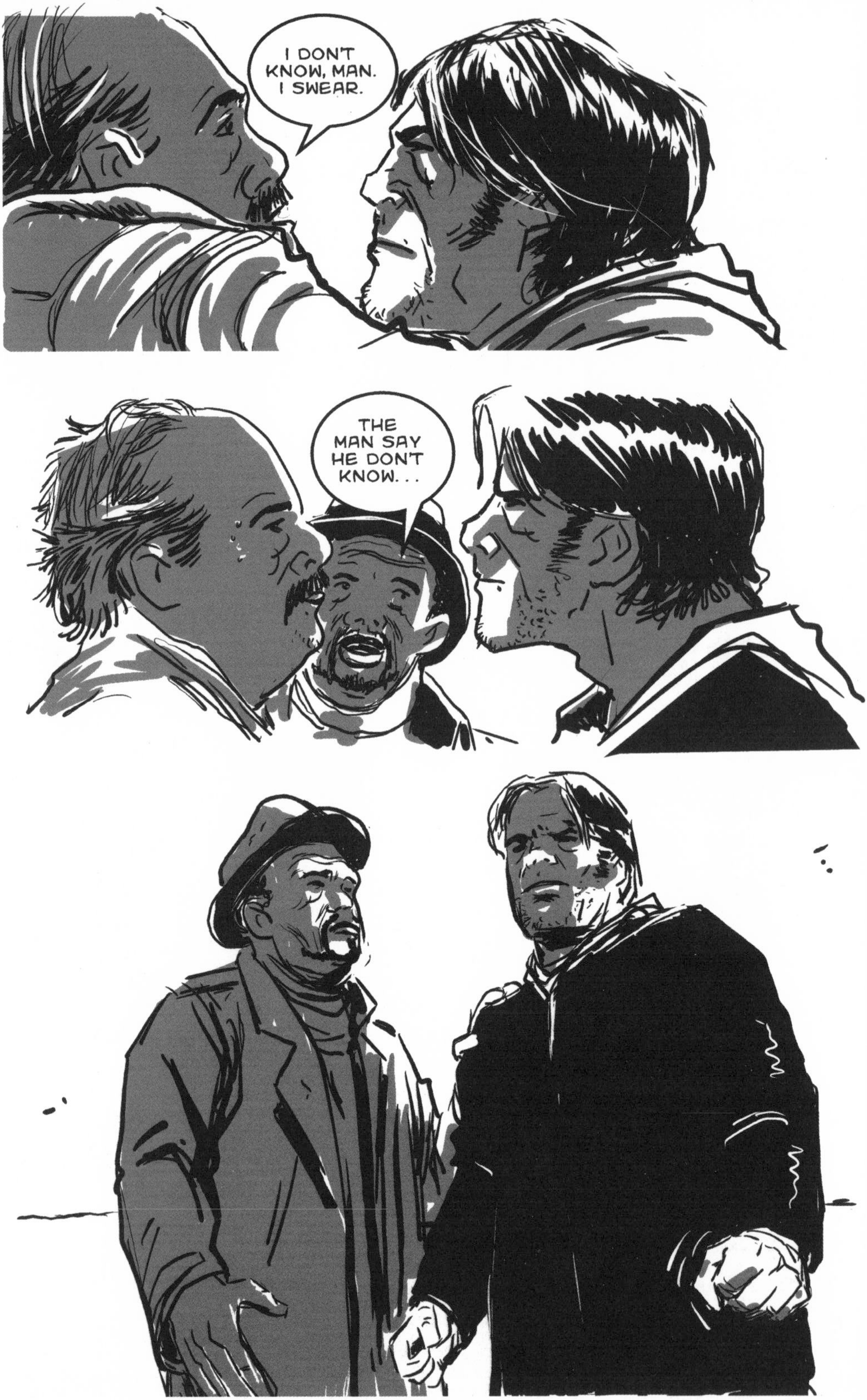
I DON'T KNOW, MAN. I SWEAR.
THE MAN SAY HE DON'T KNOW...

That afternoon I started searching all around the Quarter. I looked into any painted window using the words music, pawn, or antique.
I learned his sax was a classic from the forties, a collector's item that could pay for a dozen caskets and burial plots.

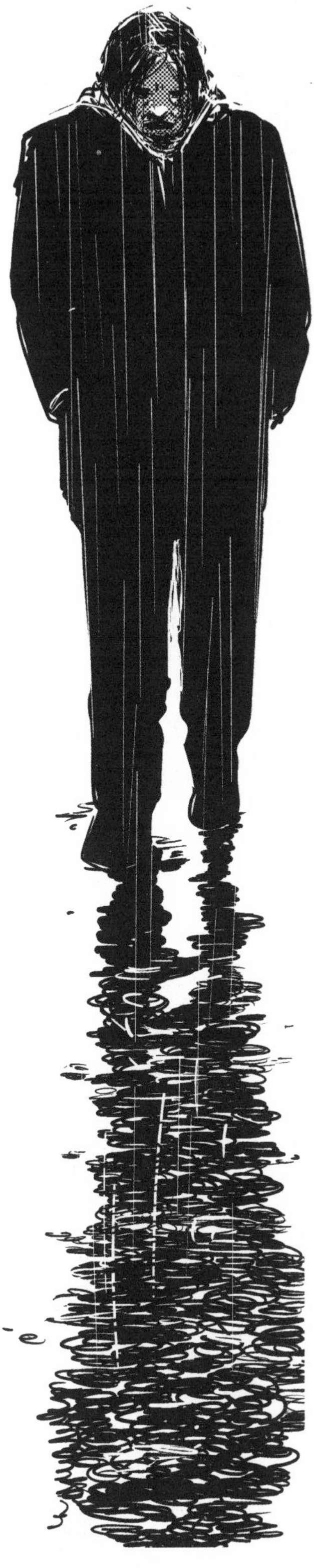

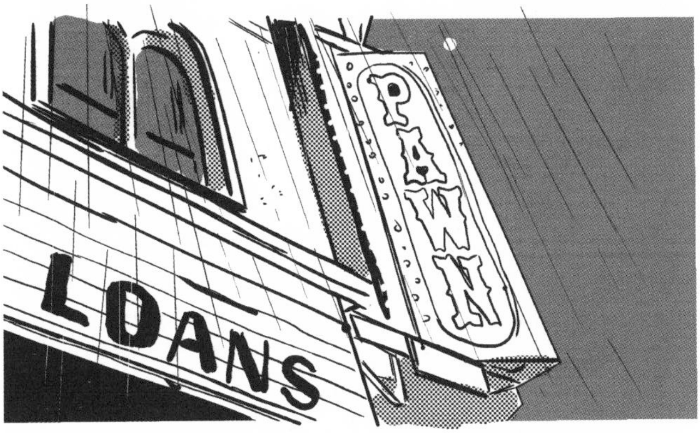
PAWN
LOANS

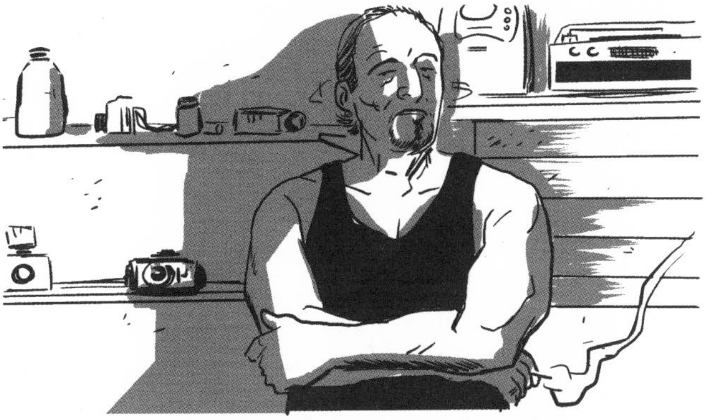

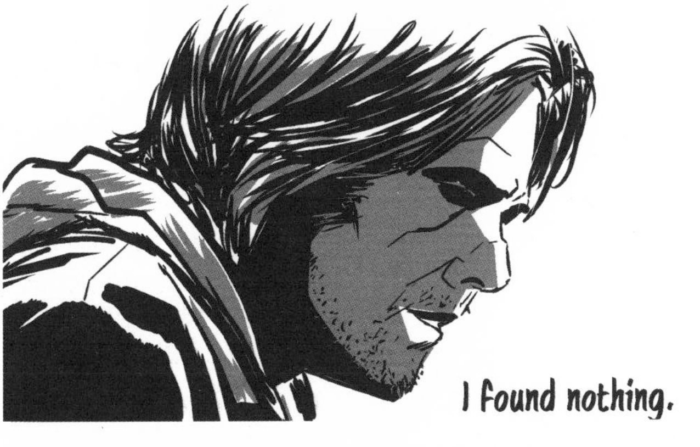
I found nothing.

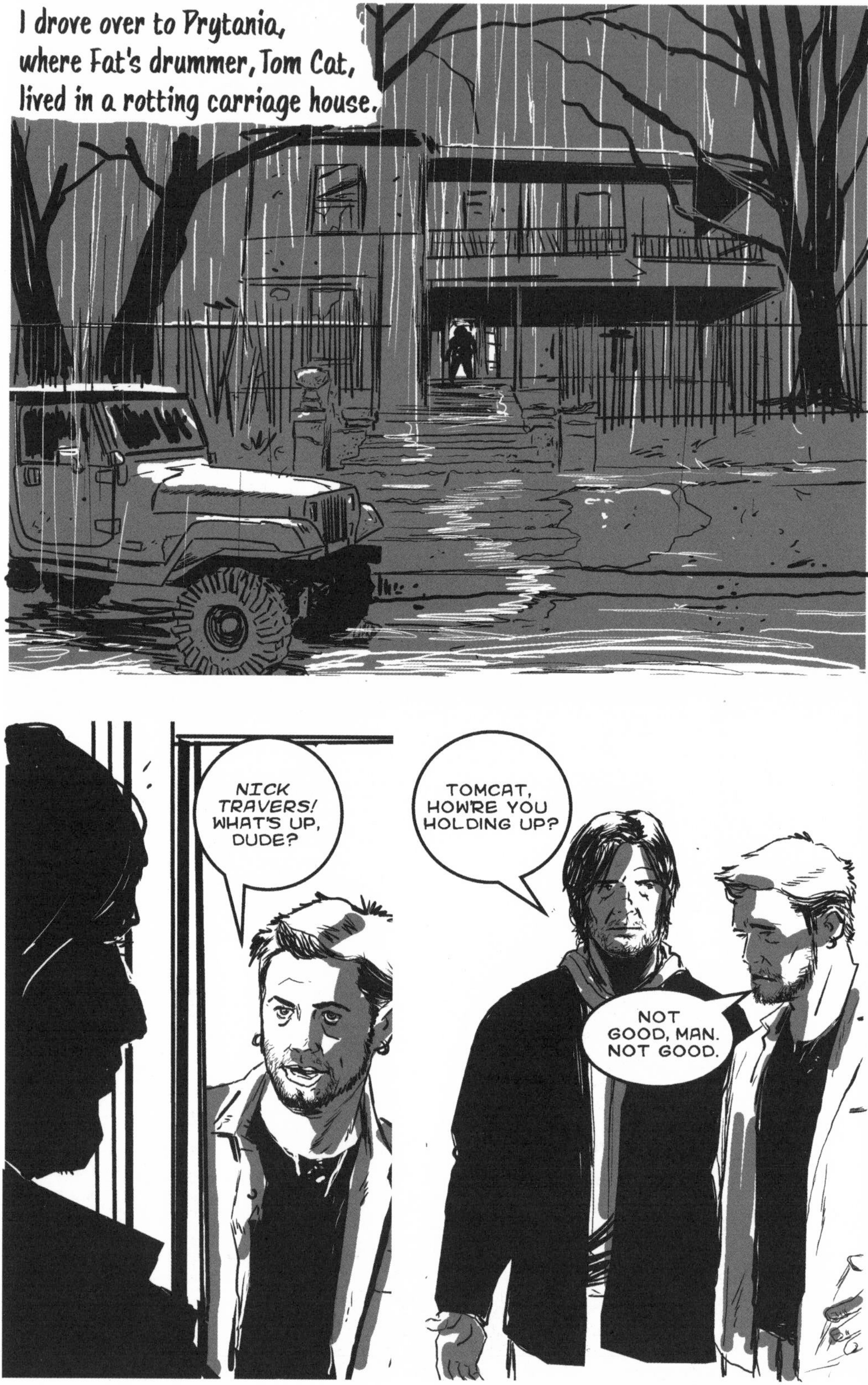
I drove over to Prytania, where Fat's drummer, Tom Cat, lived in a rotting carriage house.
NICK TRAVERS! WHAT'S UP, DUDE?
TOMCAT, HOW'RE YOU HOLDING UP?
NOT GOOD, MAN. NOT GOOD.

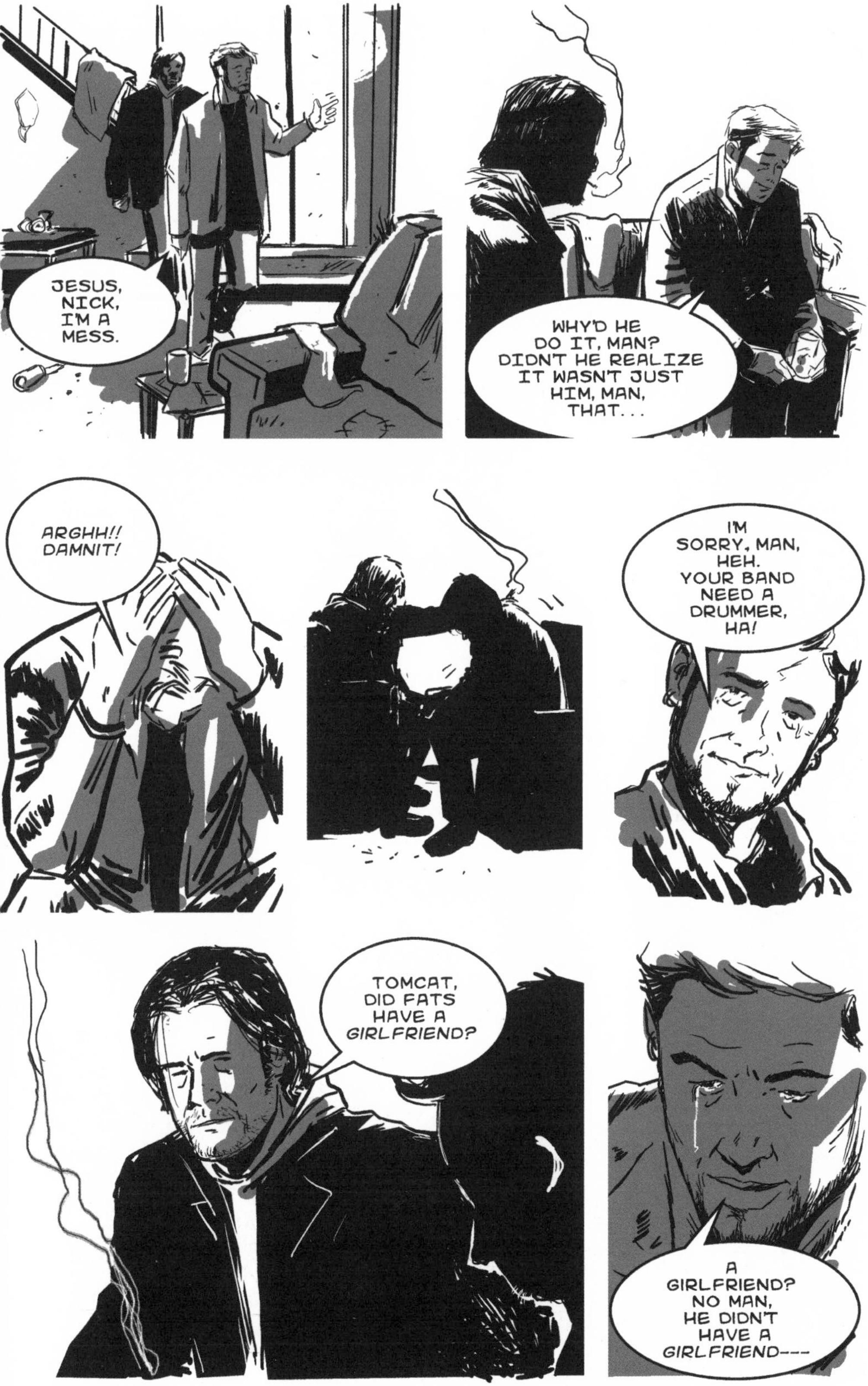
JESUS, NICK, I'M A MESS.
WHY'D HE DO IT, MAN? DIDN'T HE REALIZE IT WASN'T JUST HIM, MAN, THAT...
ARGHH!! DAMNIT!
I'M SORRY, MAN, HEH. YOUR BAND NEED A DRUMMER, HA!
TOMCAT, DID FATS HAVE A GIRLFRIEND?
A GIRLFRIEND? NO MAN, HE DIDN'T HAVE A GIRLFRIEND---

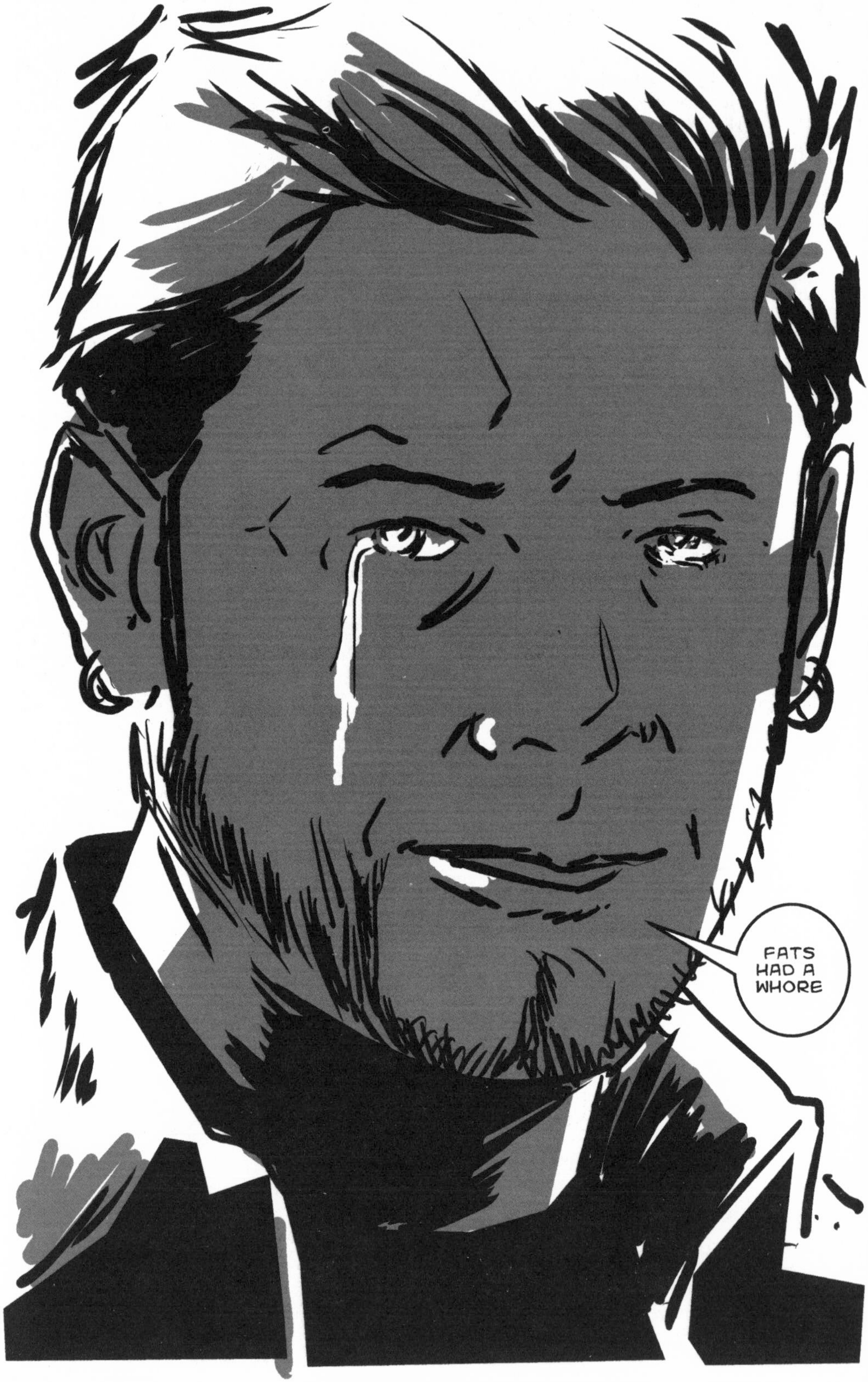
FATS
HAD A
WHORE

CHAPTER THREE

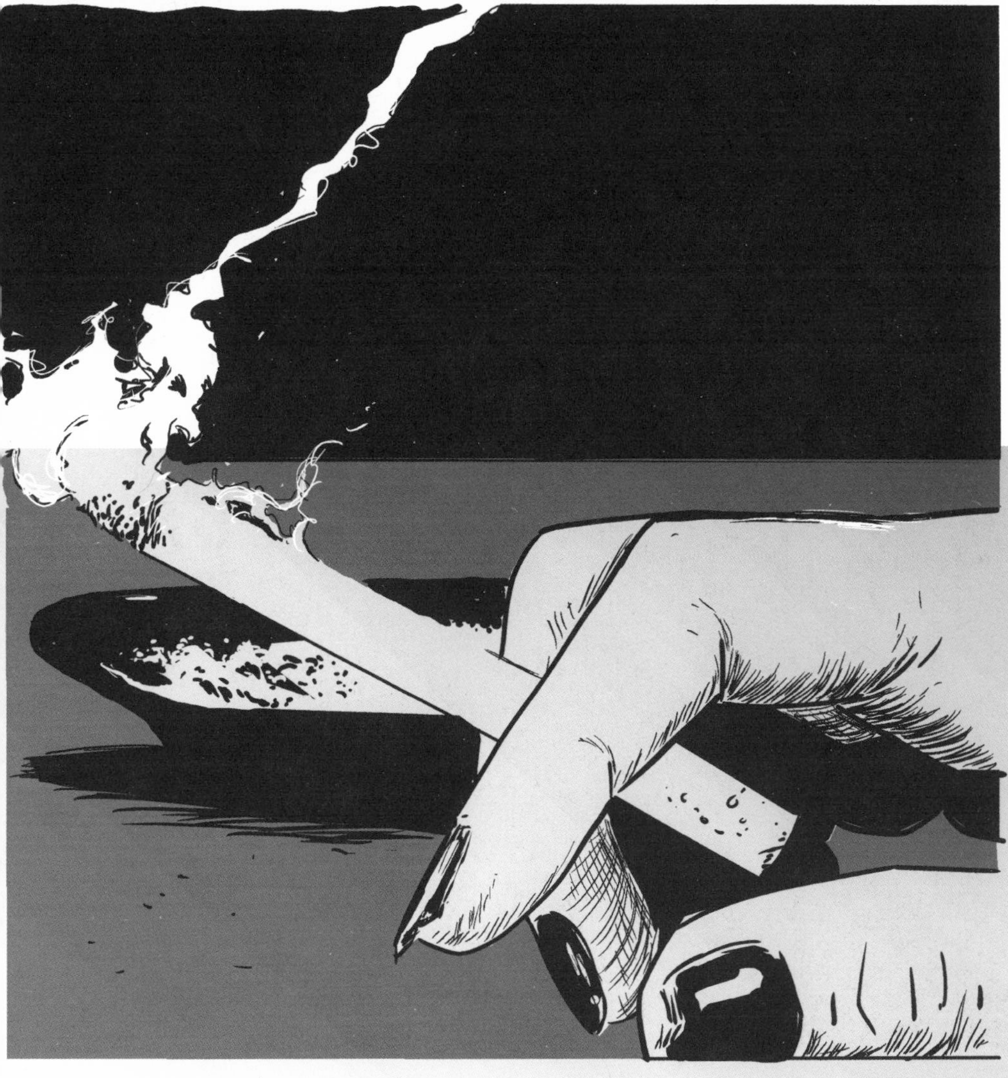

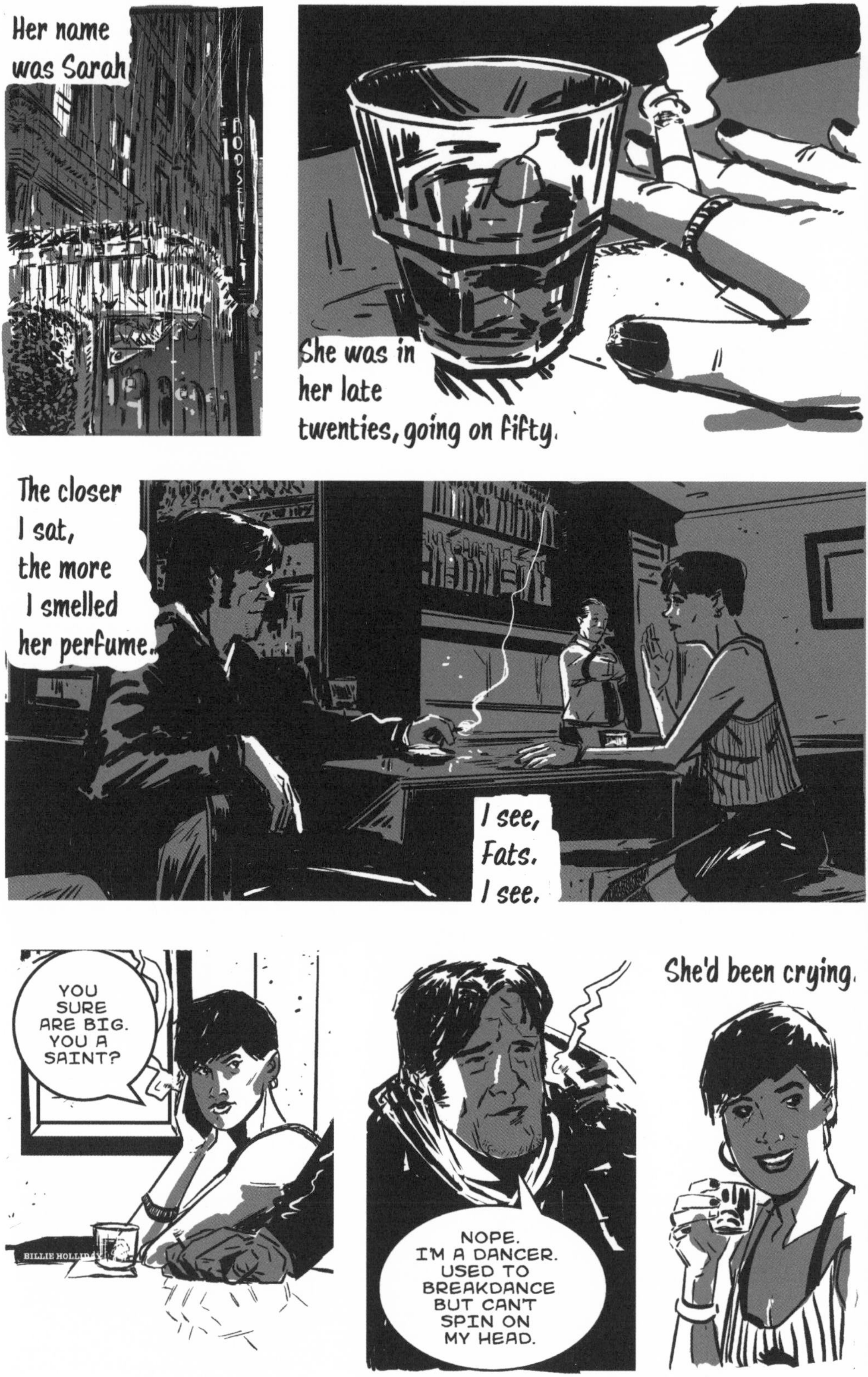
Her name was Sarah
ROOSEVELT
She was in her late twenties, going on fifty.
The closer I sat, the more I smelled her perfume...
I see, Fats. I see.
YOU SURE ARE BIG. YOU A SAINT?
BILLIE HOLLIDAY
NOPE. I'M A DANCER. USED TO BREAKDANCE BUT CAN'T SPIN ON MY HEAD.
She'd been crying.

HOW IS IT? THE BOOK?

A FRIEND GAVE IT TO ME---

HEY, SARAH. YOU READY?

OH.

WE ALREADY PAID. YOU'RE GOING TO HAVE TO DO IT YOURSELF, SON.

YOU DON'T HAVE TO DO THIS.

IT'S GONNA BE FINE. JUST FINE.

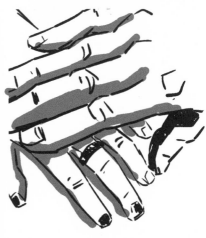

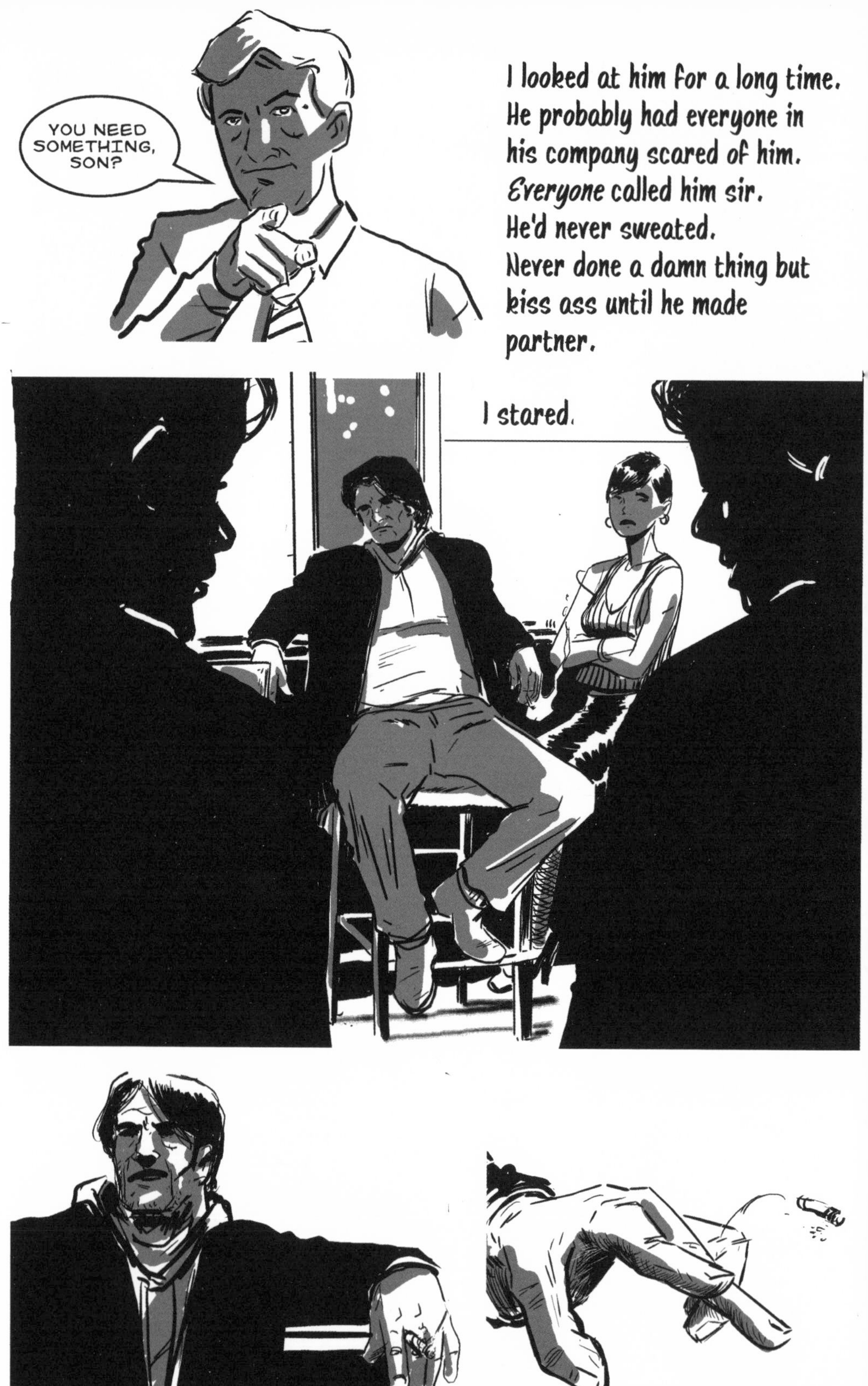
YOU NEED SOMETHING, SON?
I looked at him for a long time. He probably had everyone in his company scared of him. *Everyone* called him sir. He'd never sweated. Never done a damn thing but kiss ass until he made partner.
I stared.

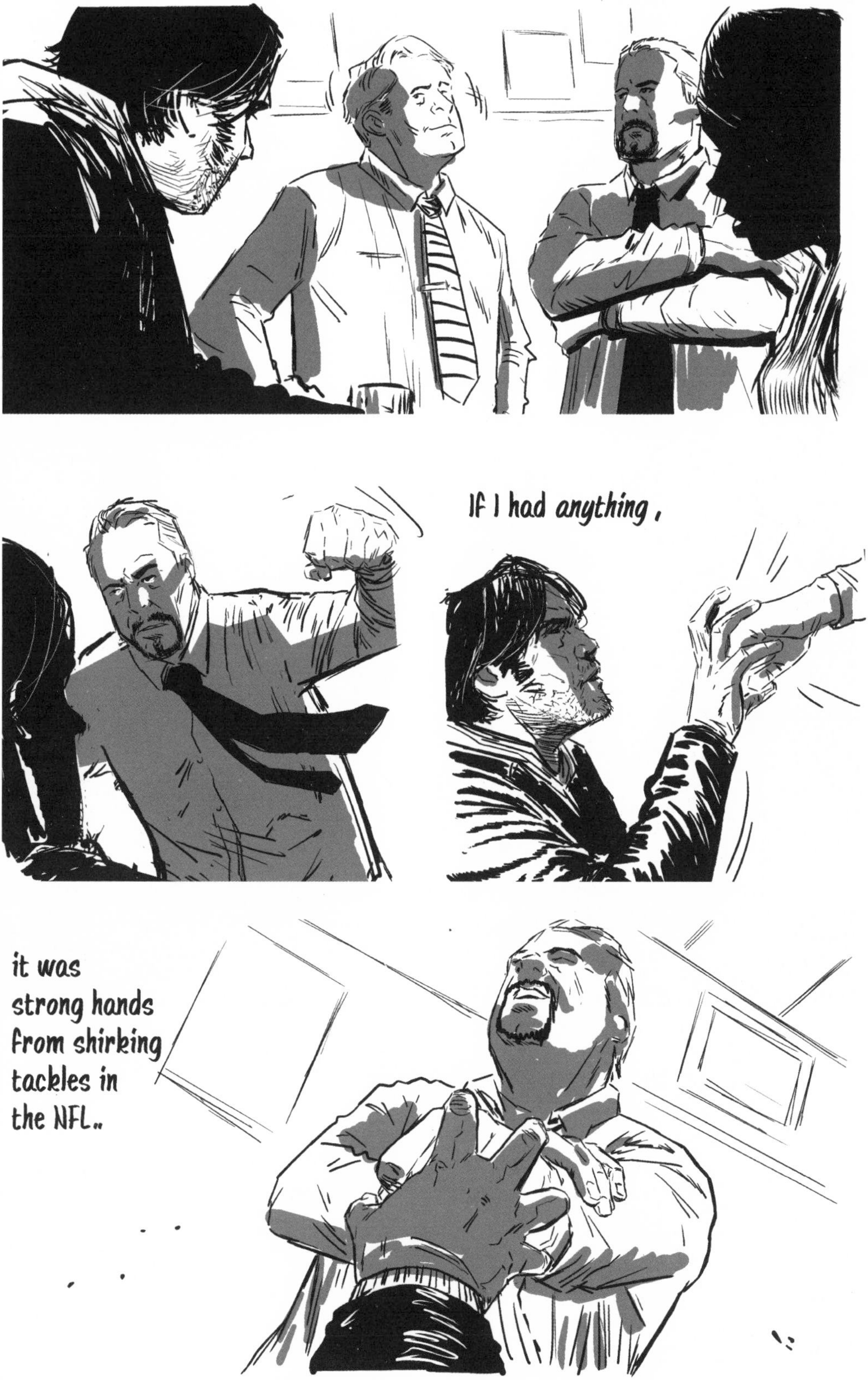
If I had anything,
it was strong hands from shirking tackles in the NFL..

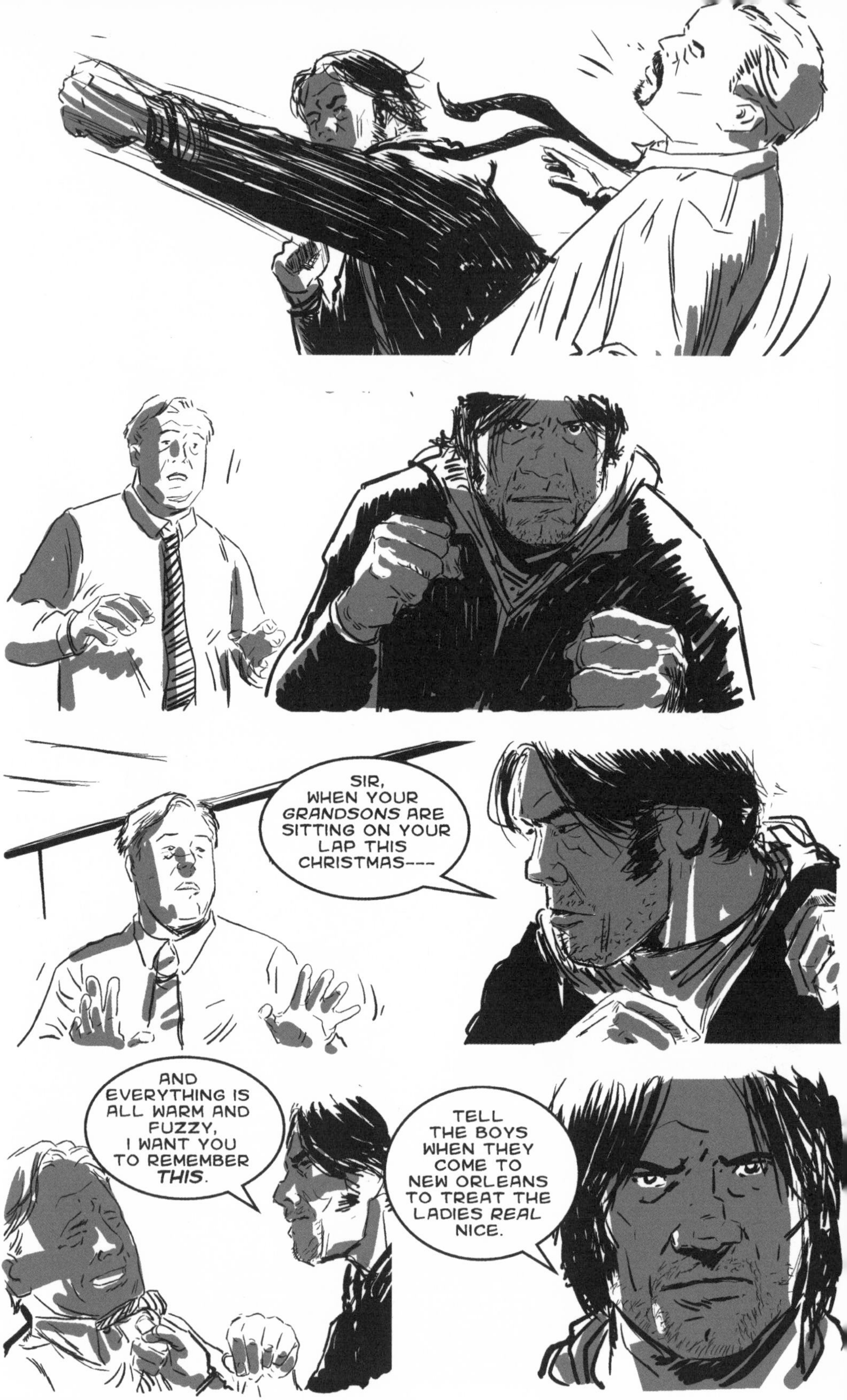
SIR, WHEN YOUR *GRANDSONS* ARE SITTING ON YOUR LAP THIS CHRISTMAS---
AND EVERYTHING IS ALL WARM AND FUZZY, I WANT YOU TO REMEMBER *THIS*.
TELL THE BOYS WHEN THEY COME TO NEW ORLEANS TO TREAT THE LADIES *REAL* NICE.

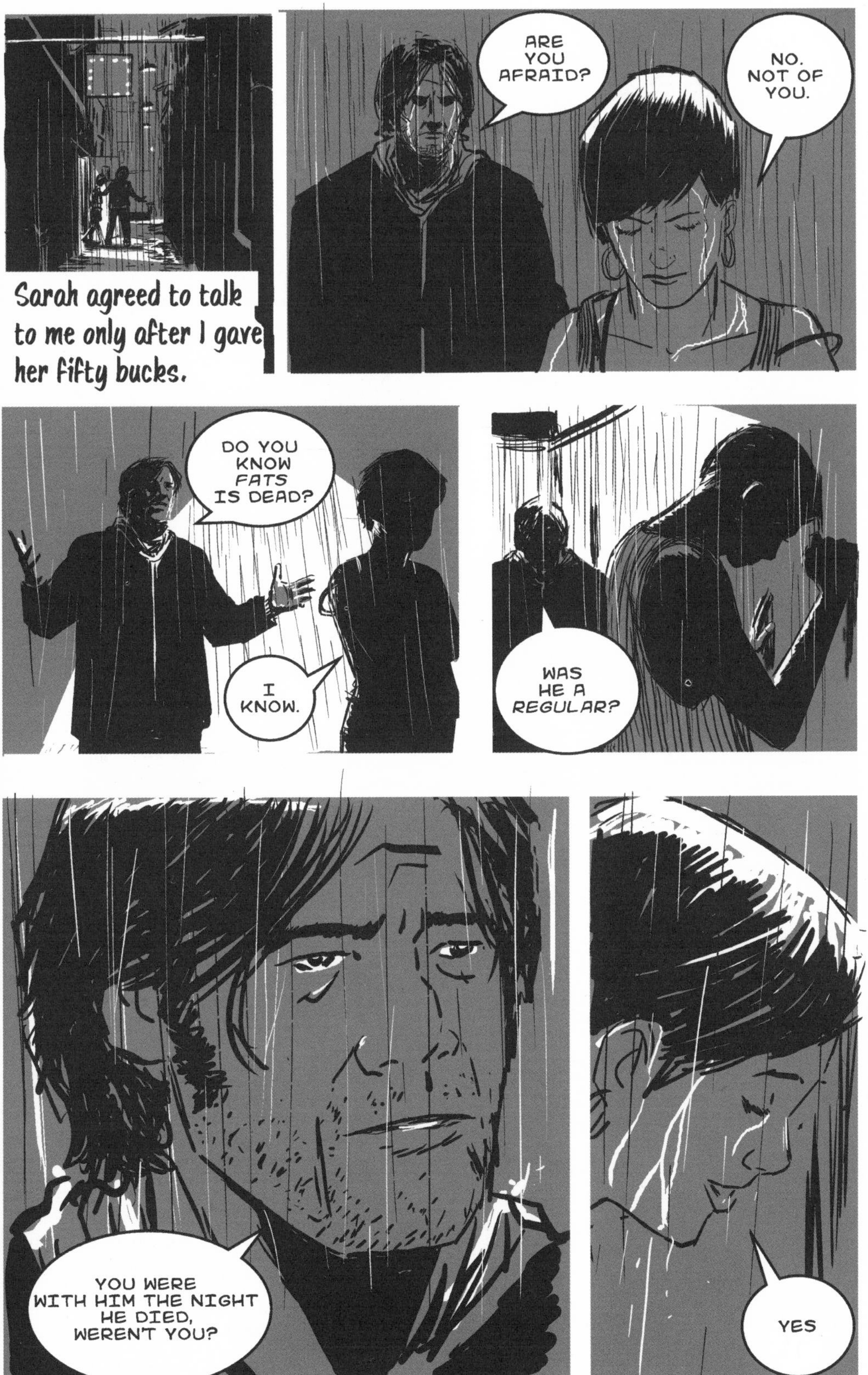
Sarah agreed to talk to me only after I gave her fifty bucks.
ARE YOU AFRAID?
NO. NOT OF YOU.
DO YOU KNOW FATS IS DEAD?
I KNOW.
WAS HE A REGULAR?
YOU WERE WITH HIM THE NIGHT HE DIED, WEREN'T YOU?
YES

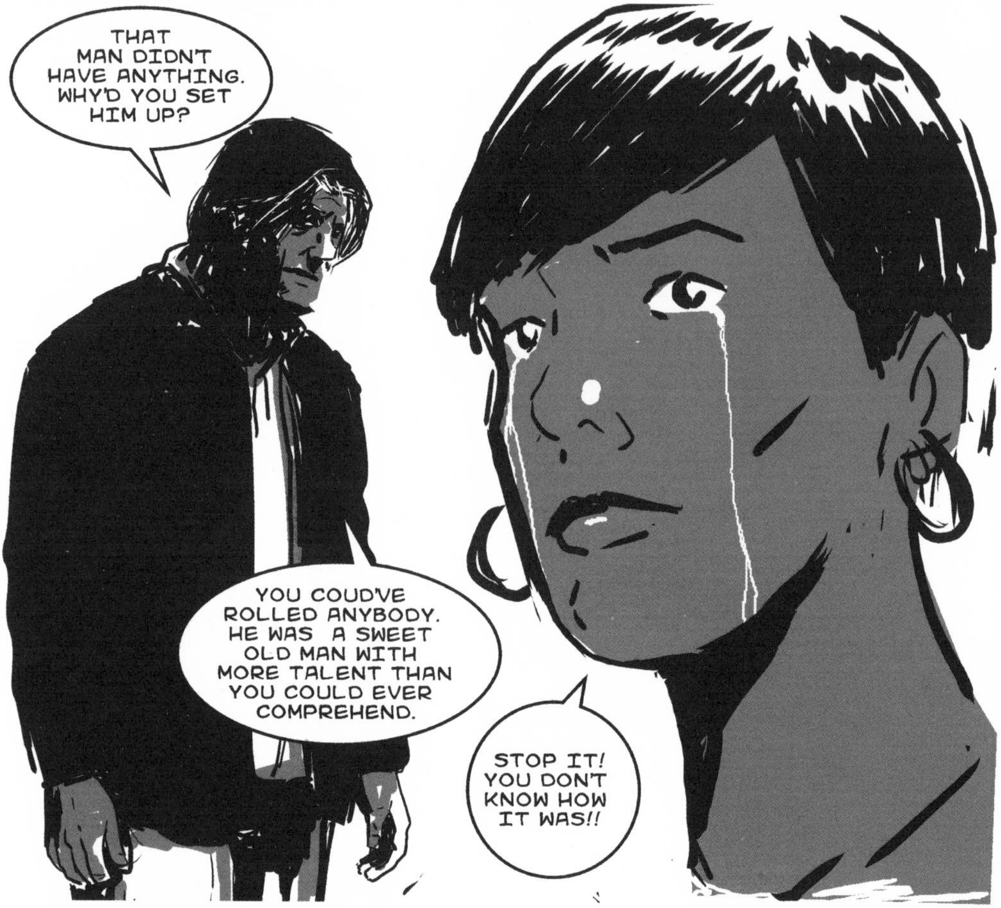
THAT MAN DIDN'T HAVE ANYTHING. WHY'D YOU SET HIM UP?
YOU COUD'VE ROLLED ANYBODY. HE WAS A SWEET OLD MAN WITH MORE TALENT THAN YOU COULD EVER COMPREHEND.
STOP IT! YOU DON'T KNOW HOW IT WAS!!

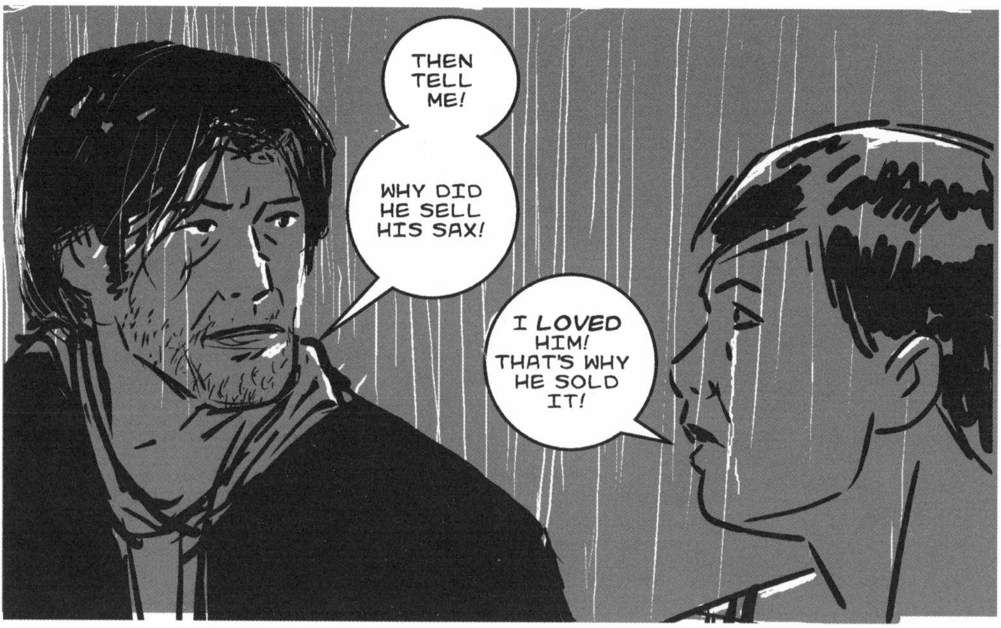
THEN TELL ME!
WHY DID HE SELL HIS SAX!
I *LOVED* HIM! THAT'S WHY HE SOLD IT!

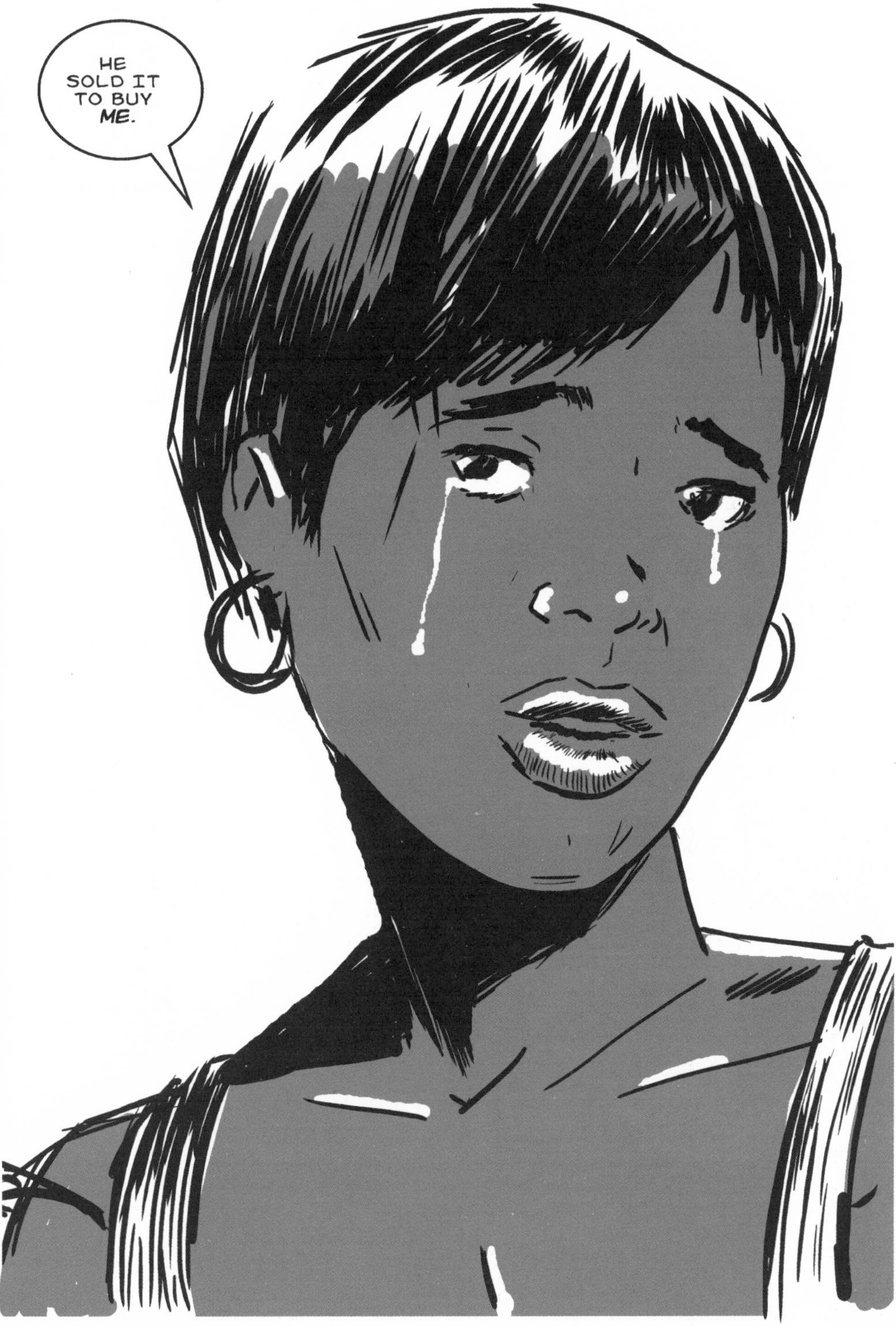
HE SOLD IT TO BUY ME.

CHAPTER FOUR

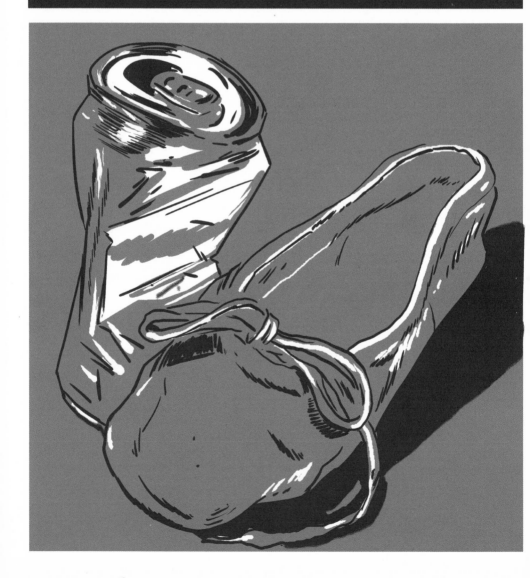

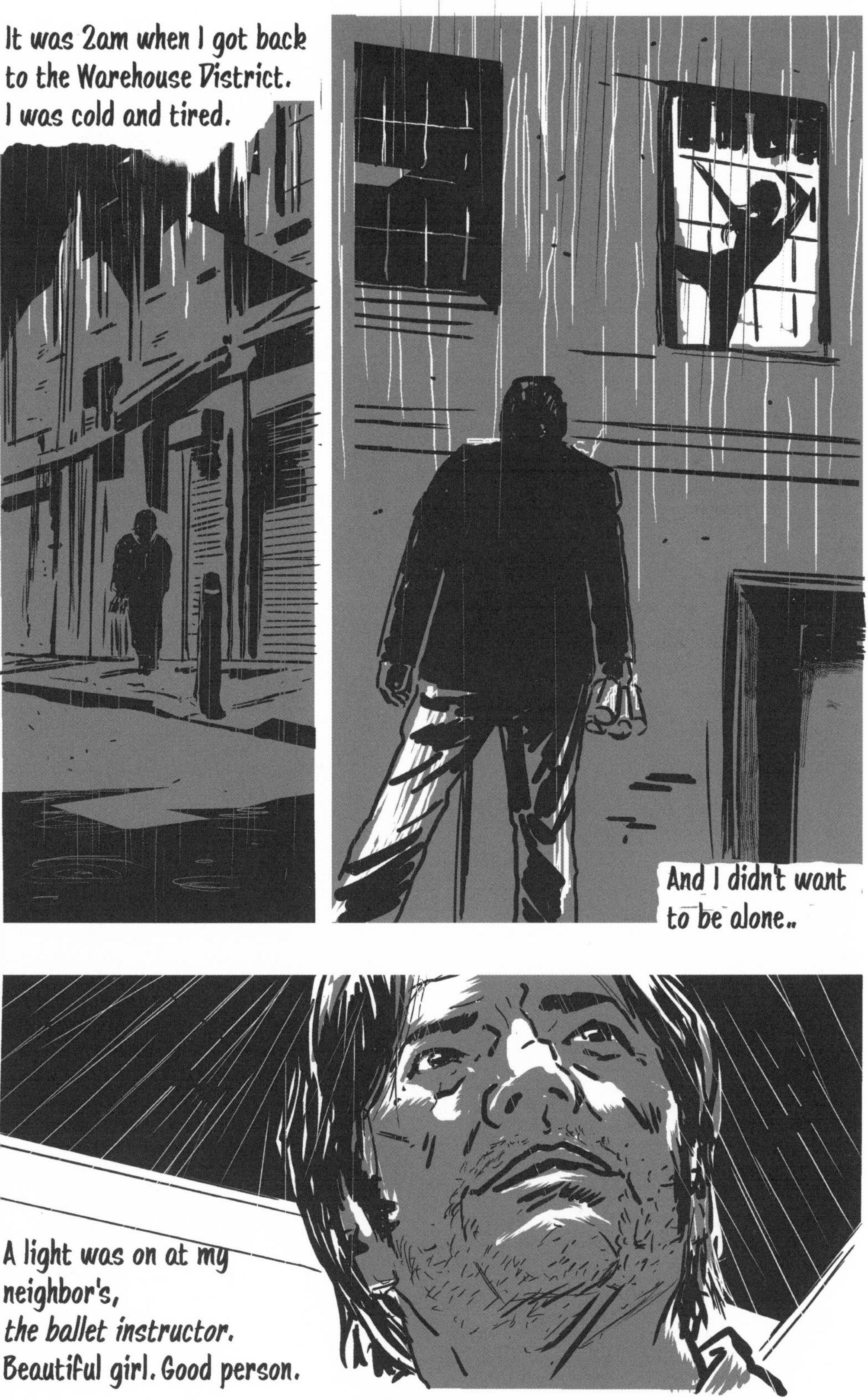
It was 2am when I got back to the Warehouse District.
I was cold and tired.
And I didn't want to be alone..
A light was on at my neighbor's,
the ballet instructor.
Beautiful girl. Good person.

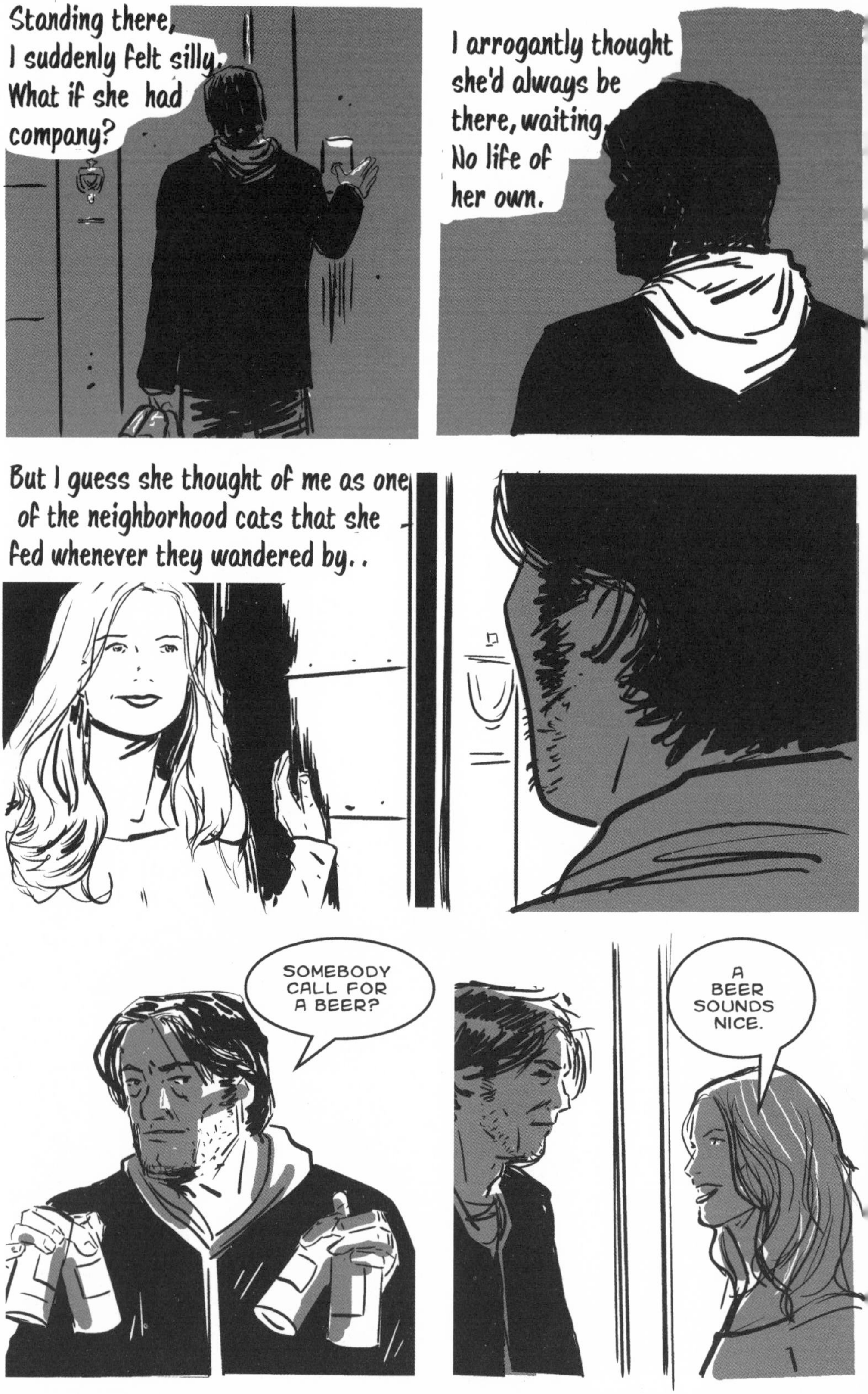

Standing there, I suddenly felt silly. What if she had company?
I arrogantly thought she'd always be there, waiting. No life of her own.
But I guess she thought of me as one of the neighborhood cats that she fed whenever they wandered by. .
SOMEBODY CALL FOR A BEER?
A BEER SOUNDS NICE.

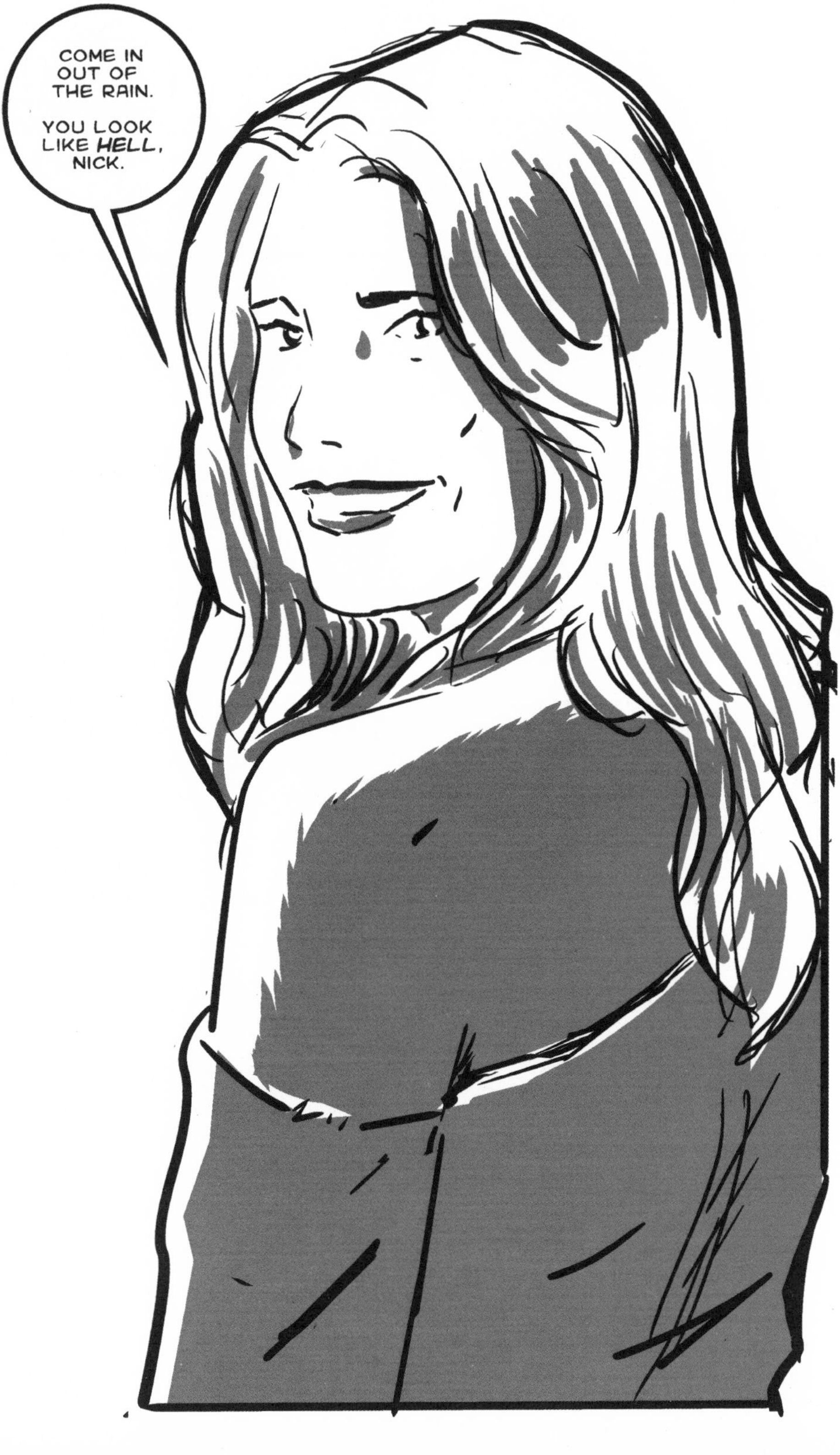
COME IN OUT OF THE RAIN.
YOU LOOK LIKE **HELL**, NICK.

CHAPTER FIVE

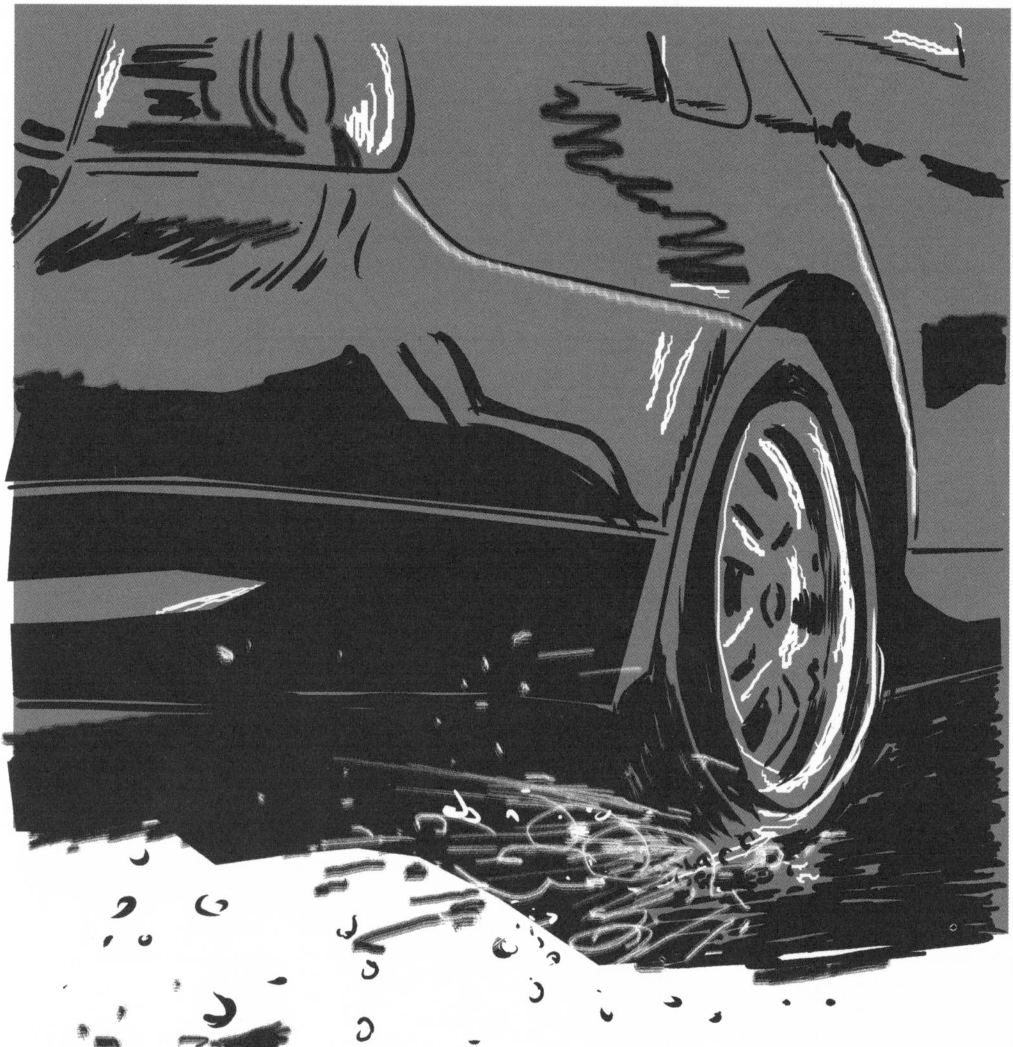

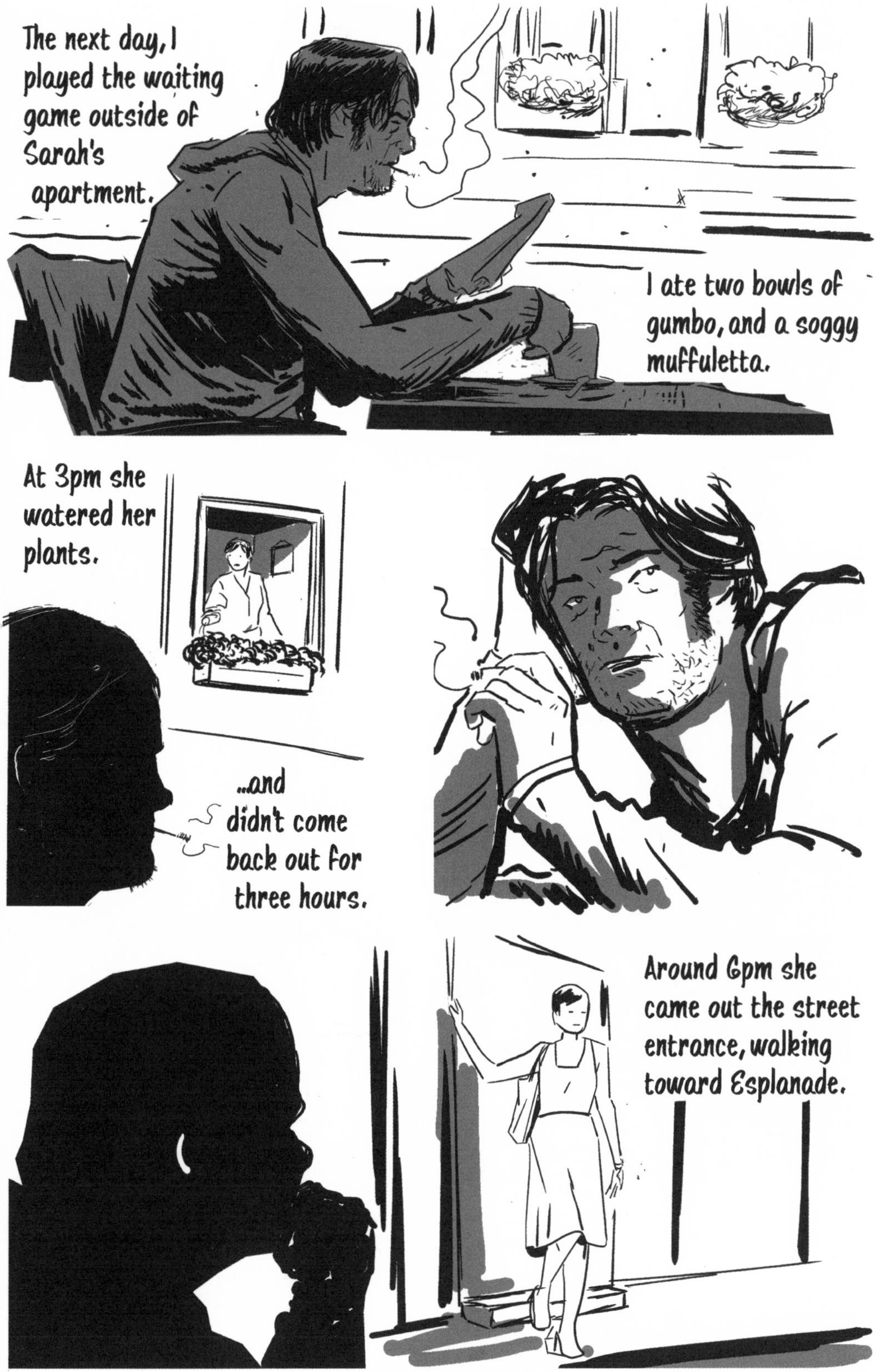
The next day, I played the waiting game outside of Sarah's apartment.
I ate two bowls of gumbo, and a soggy muffuletta.
At 3pm she watered her plants.
...and didn't come back out for three hours.
Around 6pm she came out the street entrance, walking toward Esplanade.

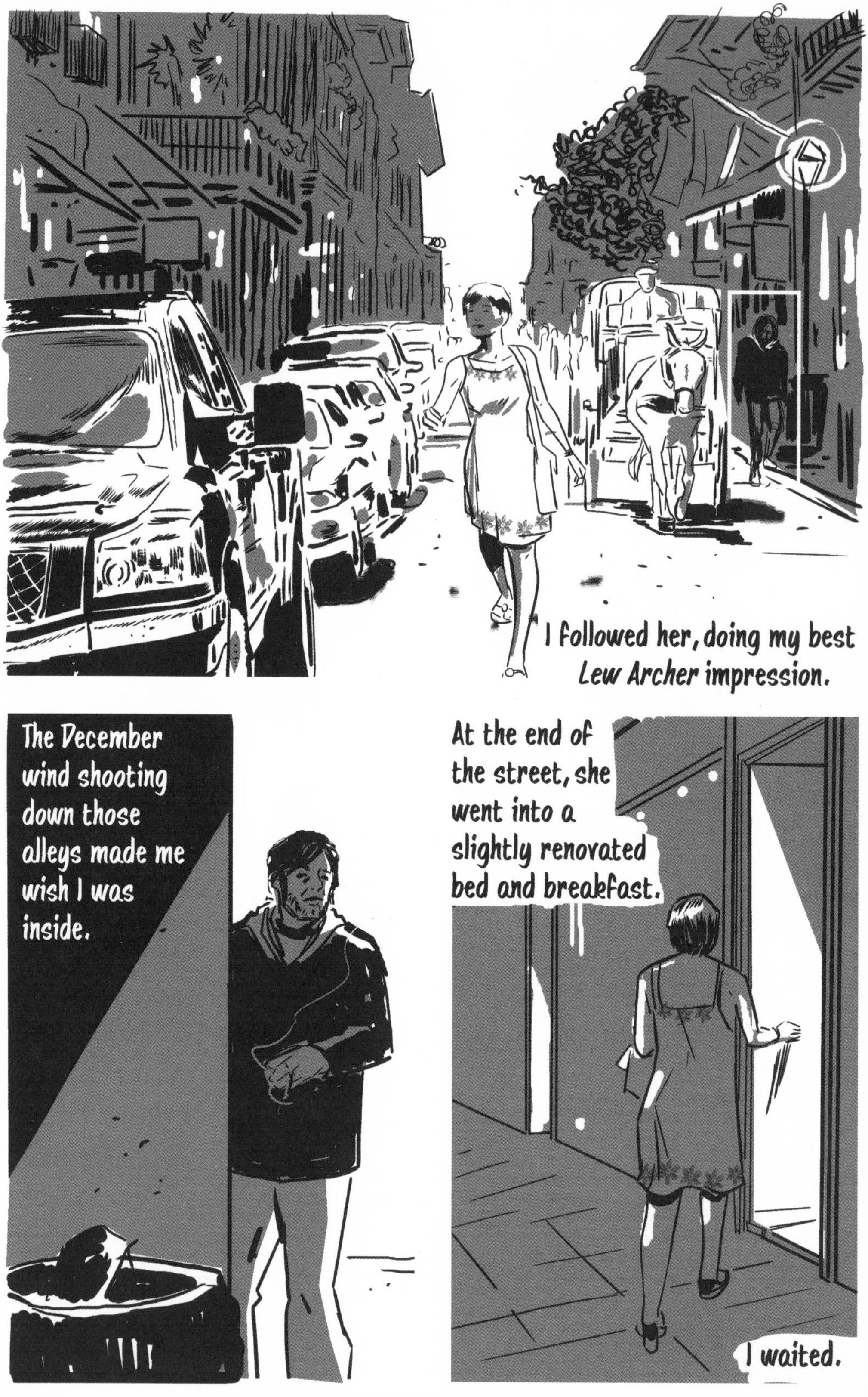
I followed her, doing my best *Lew Archer* impression.
The December wind shooting down those alleys made me wish I was inside.
At the end of the street, she went into a slightly renovated bed and breakfast.
I waited.

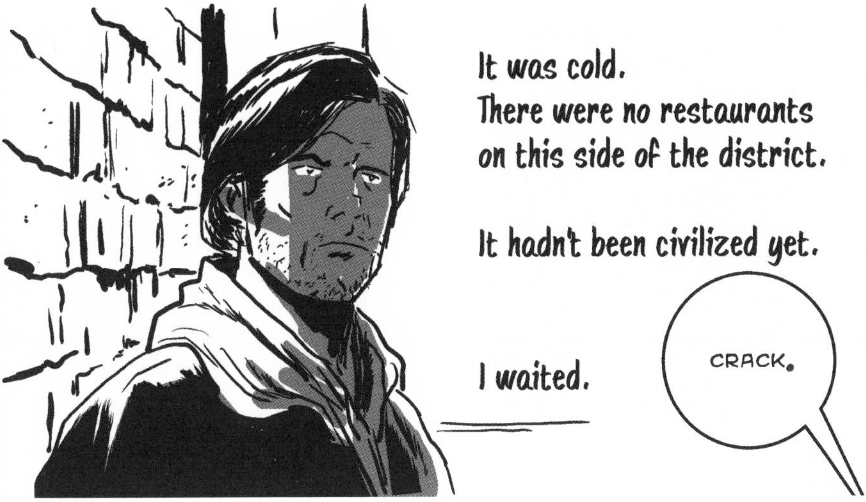
It was cold.
There were no restaurants
on this side of the district.
It hadn't been civilized yet.
I waited.
CRACK.

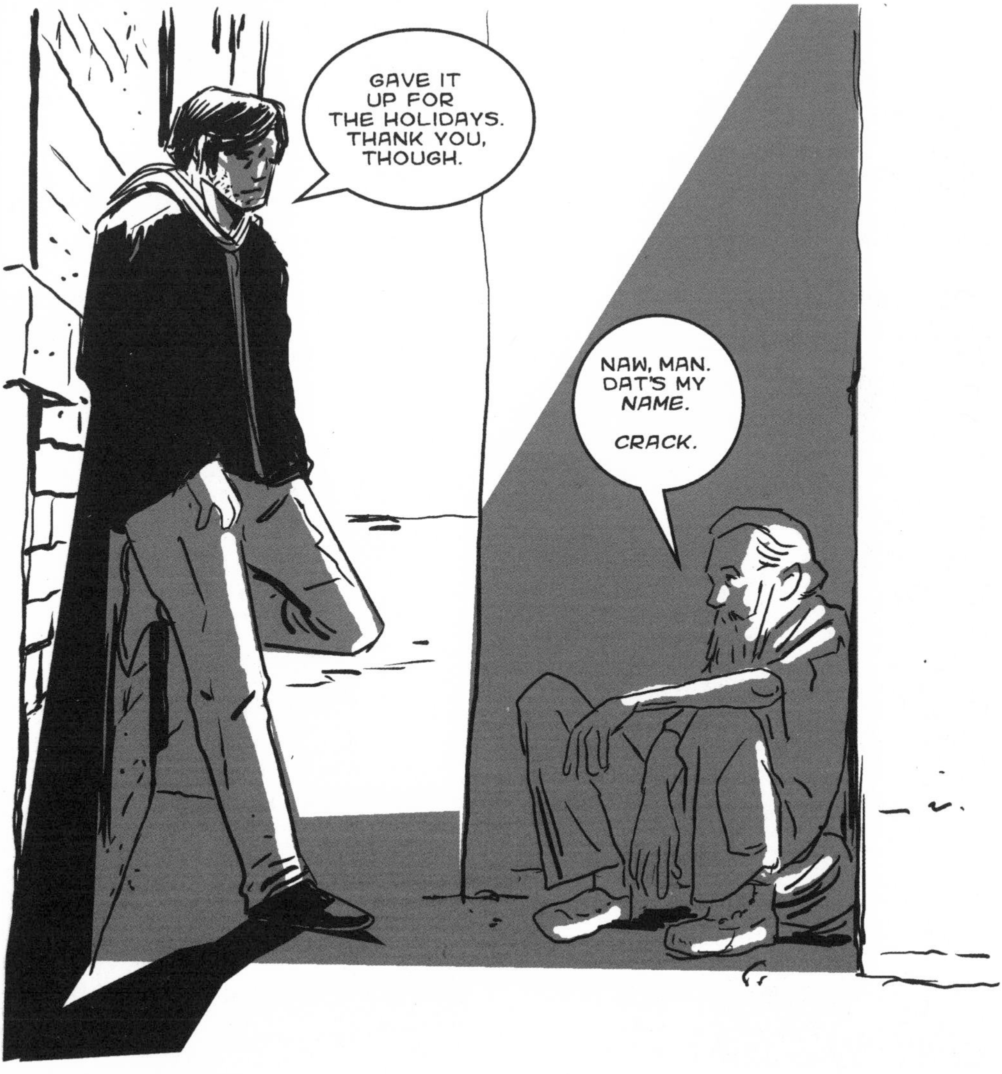
GAVE IT UP FOR THE HOLIDAYS. THANK YOU, THOUGH.
NAW, MAN. DAT'S MY NAME.
CRACK.

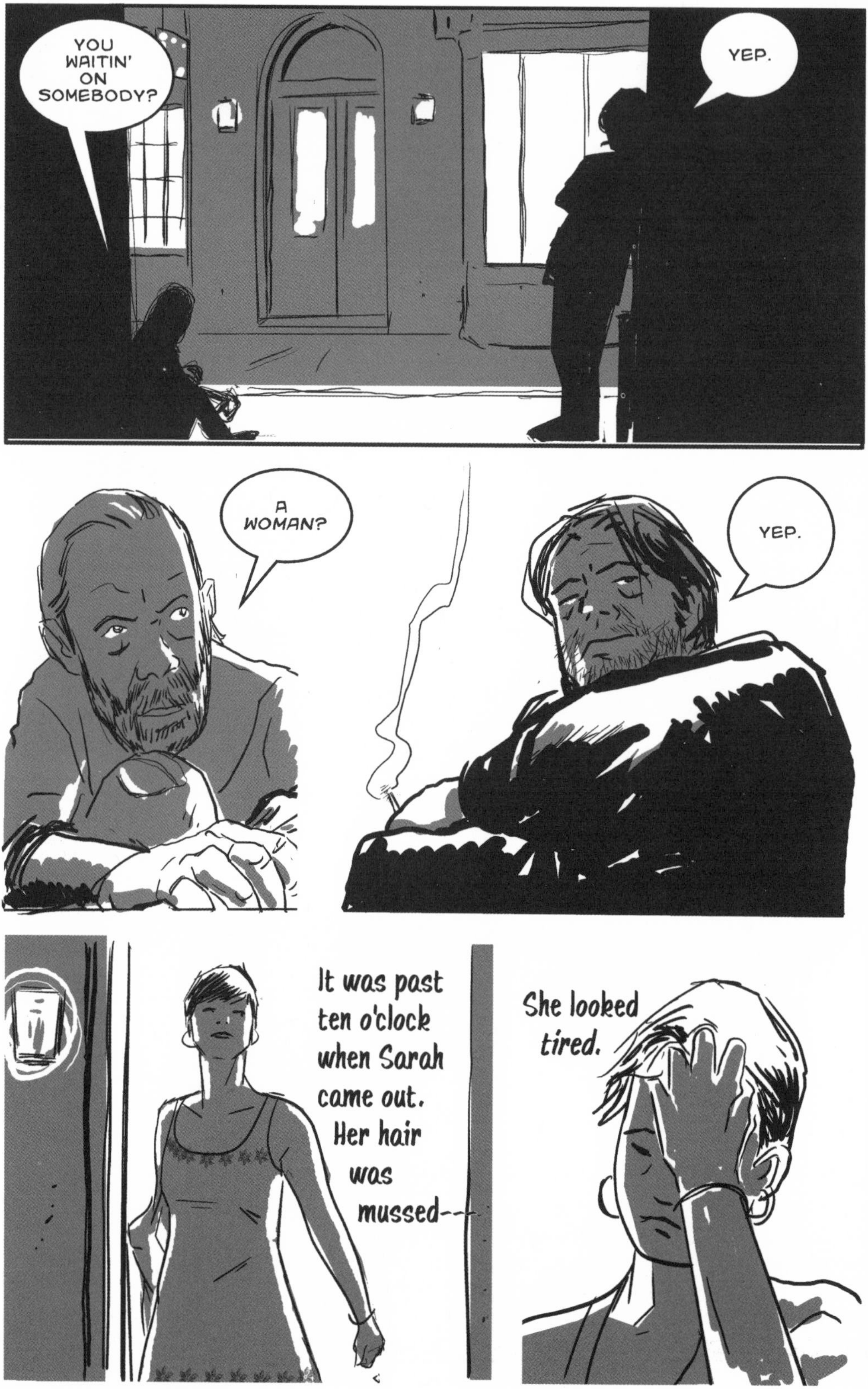
YOU WAITIN' ON SOMEBODY?
YEP.
A WOMAN?
YEP.
It was past ten o'clock when Sarah came out. Her hair was mussed--
She looked tired.

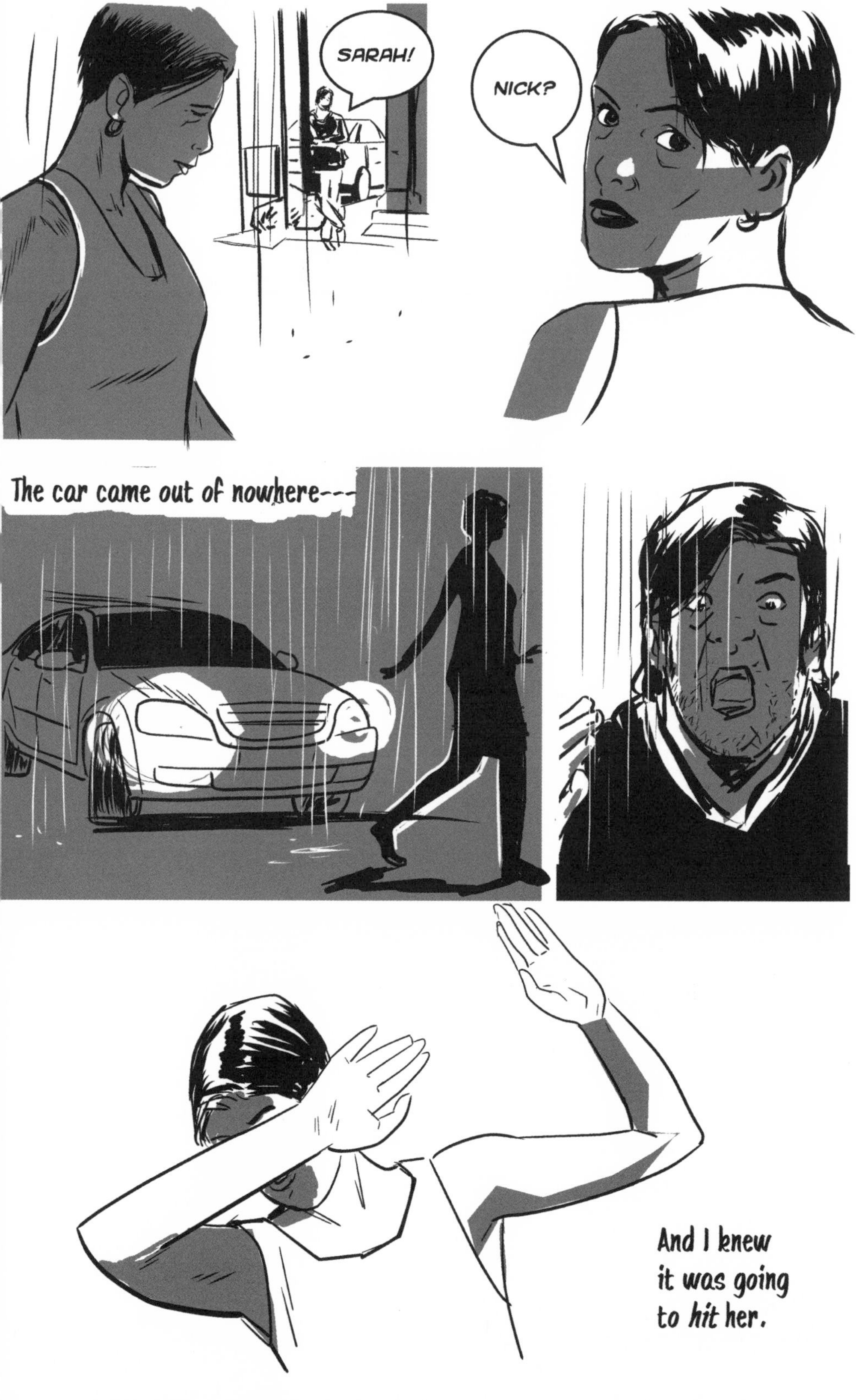
SARAH!
NICK?
The car came out of nowhere---
And I knew it was going to *hit* her.

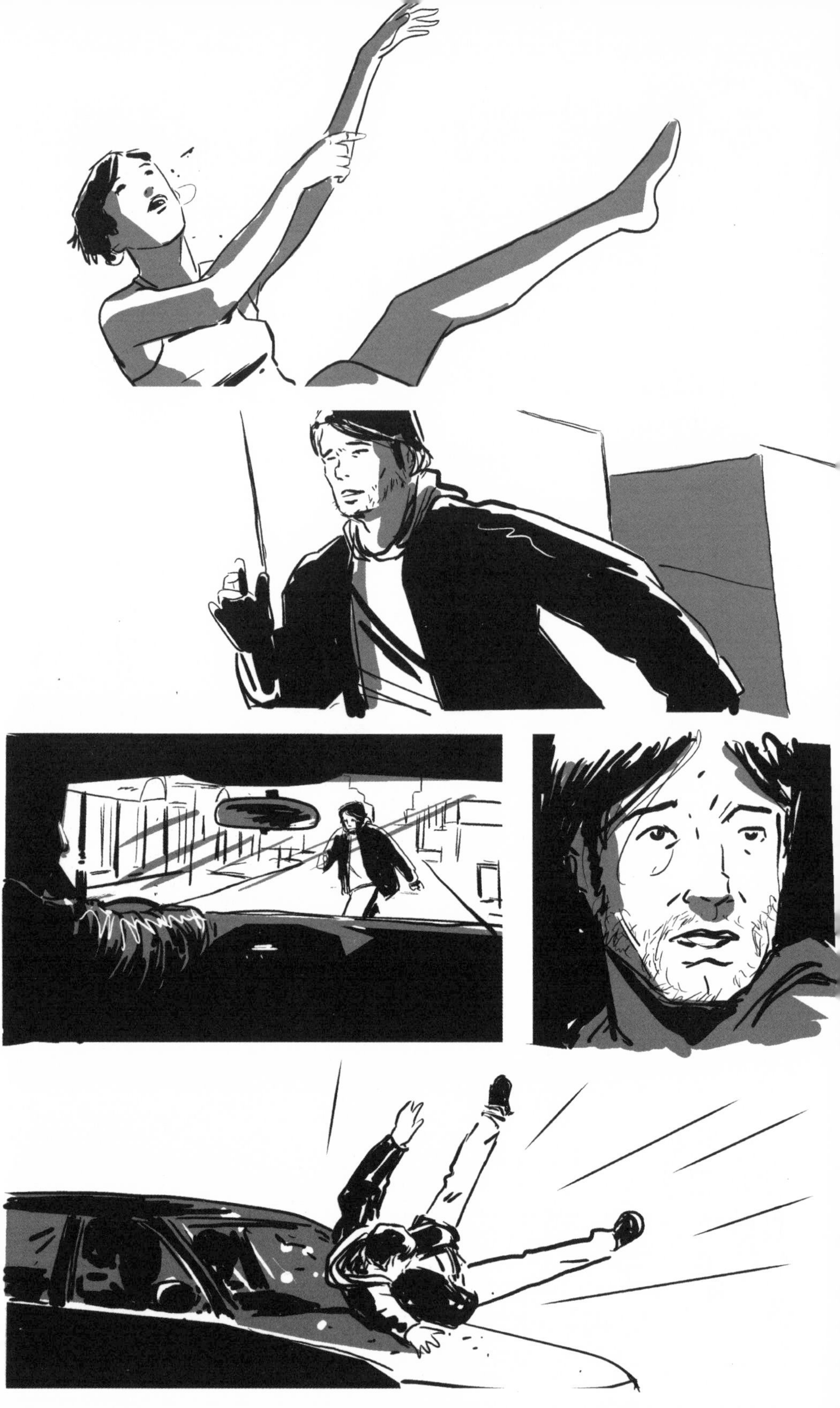

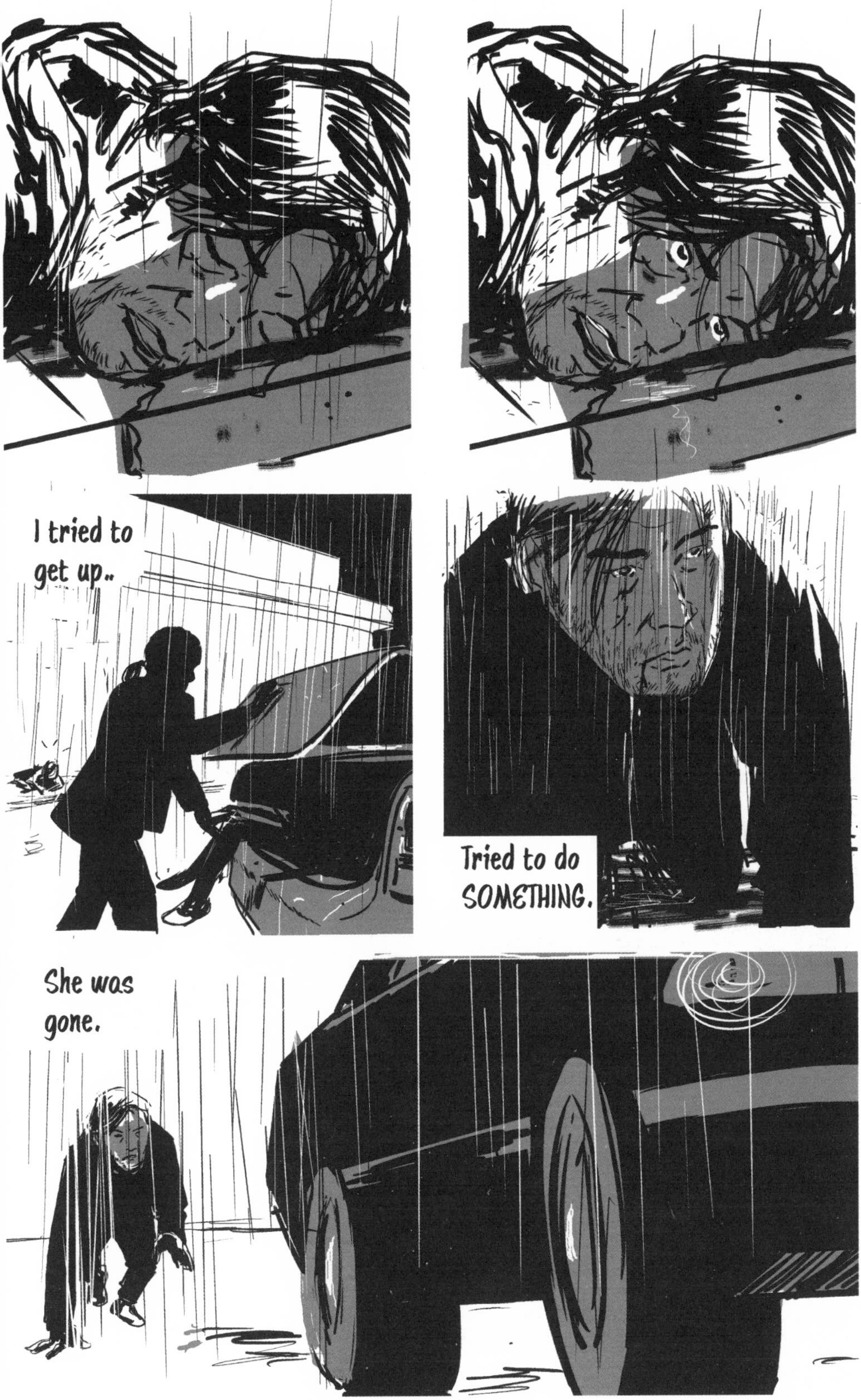

I tried to get up..
Tried to do SOMETHING.
She was gone.

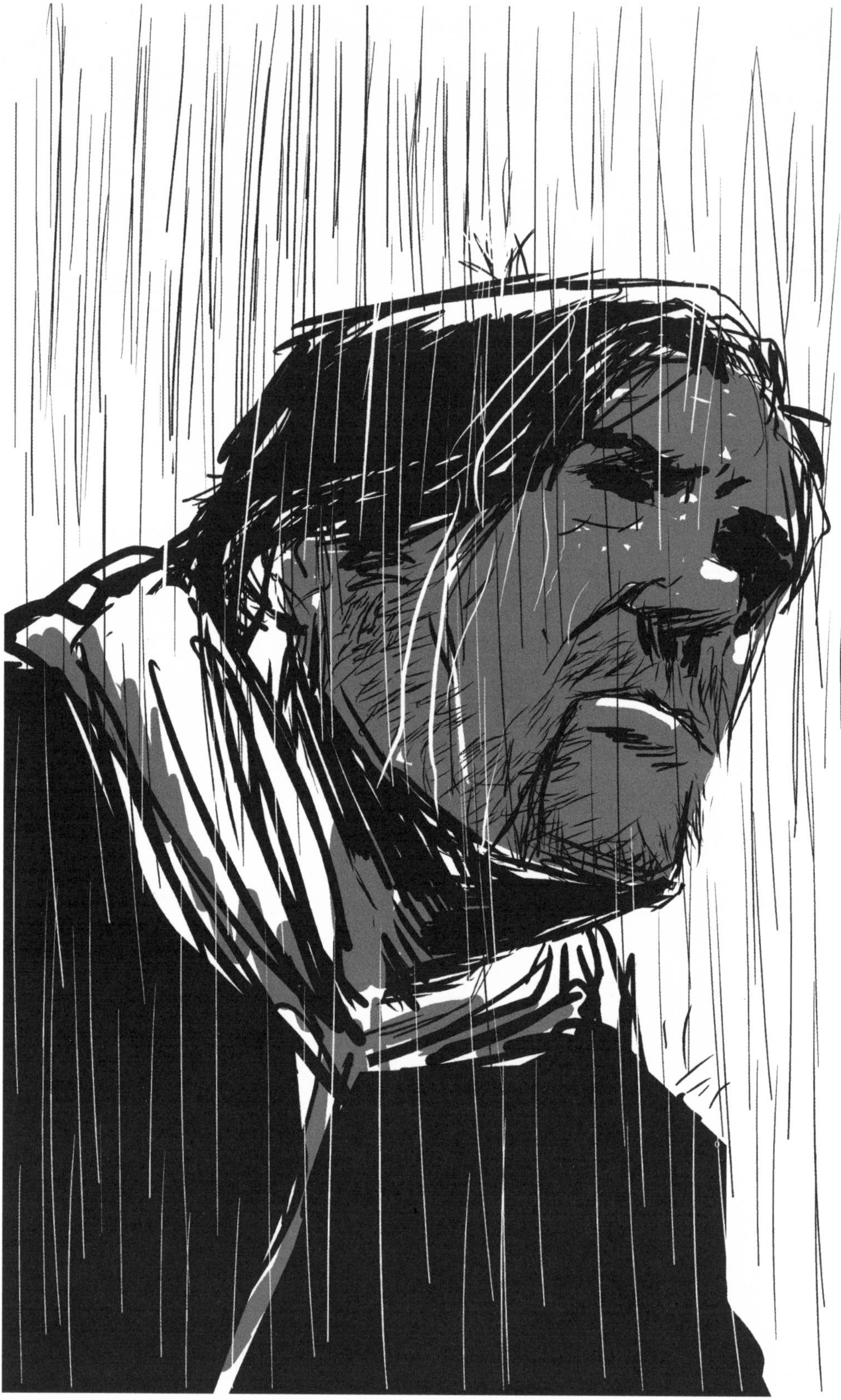

CHAPTER SIX

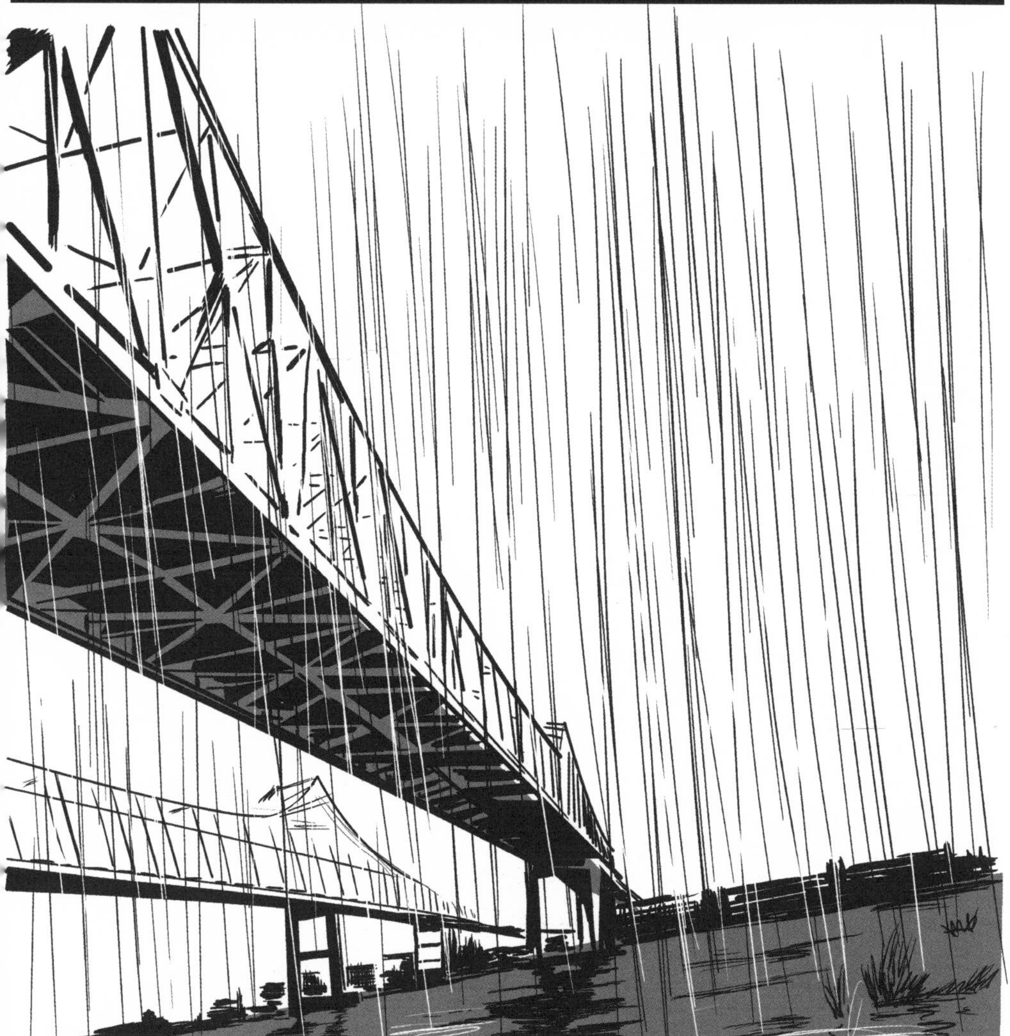

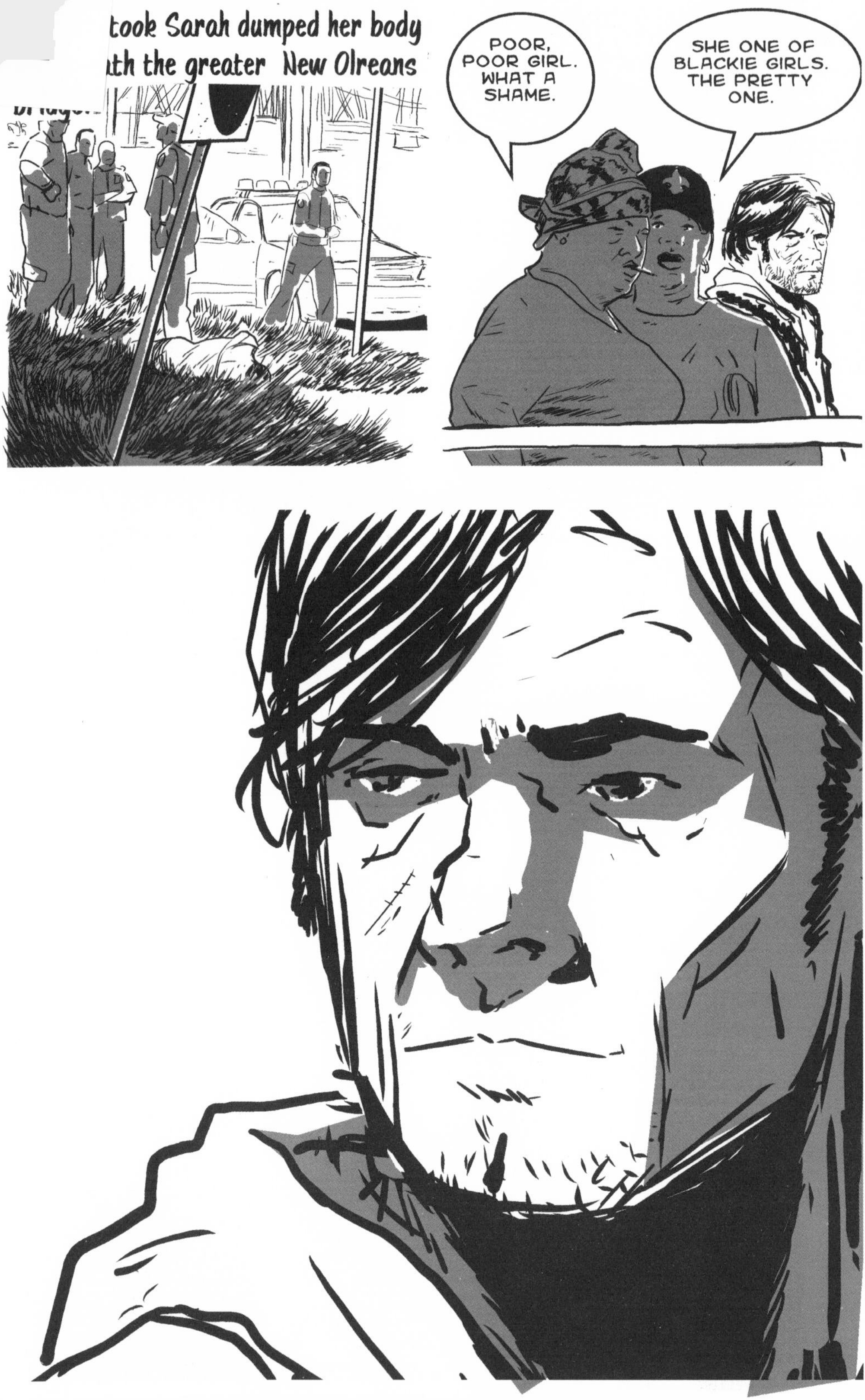
took Sarah dumped her body
ath the greater New Olreans
POOR, POOR GIRL. WHAT A SHAME.
SHE ONE OF BLACKIE GIRLS. THE PRETTY ONE.

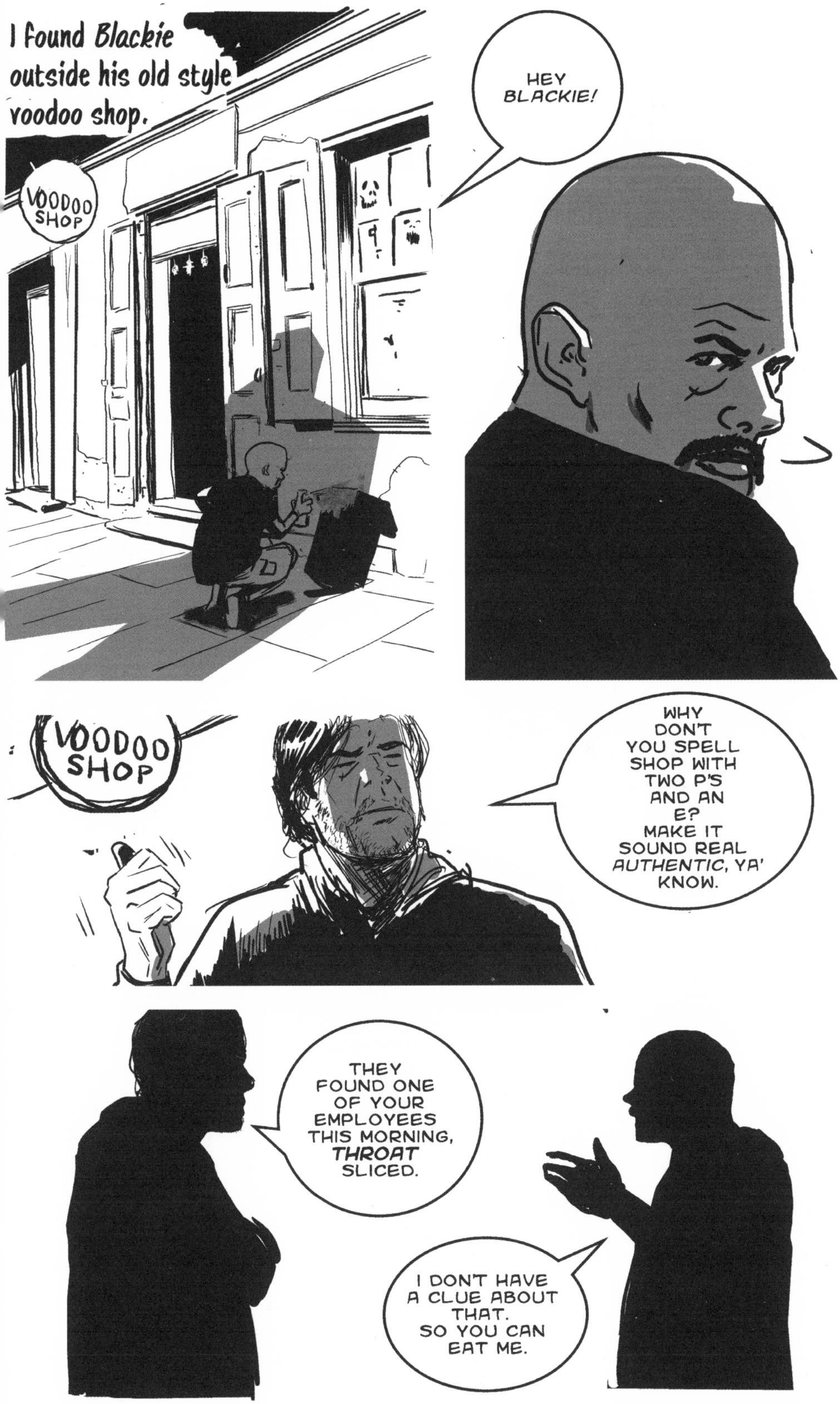
I found Blackie outside his old style voodoo shop.
VOODOO SHOP
HEY BLACKIE!
VOODOO SHOP
WHY DON'T YOU SPELL SHOP WITH TWO P'S AND AN E? MAKE IT SOUND REAL AUTHENTIC, YA' KNOW.
THEY FOUND ONE OF YOUR EMPLOYEES THIS MORNING, THROAT SLICED.
I DON'T HAVE A CLUE ABOUT THAT. SO YOU CAN EAT ME.

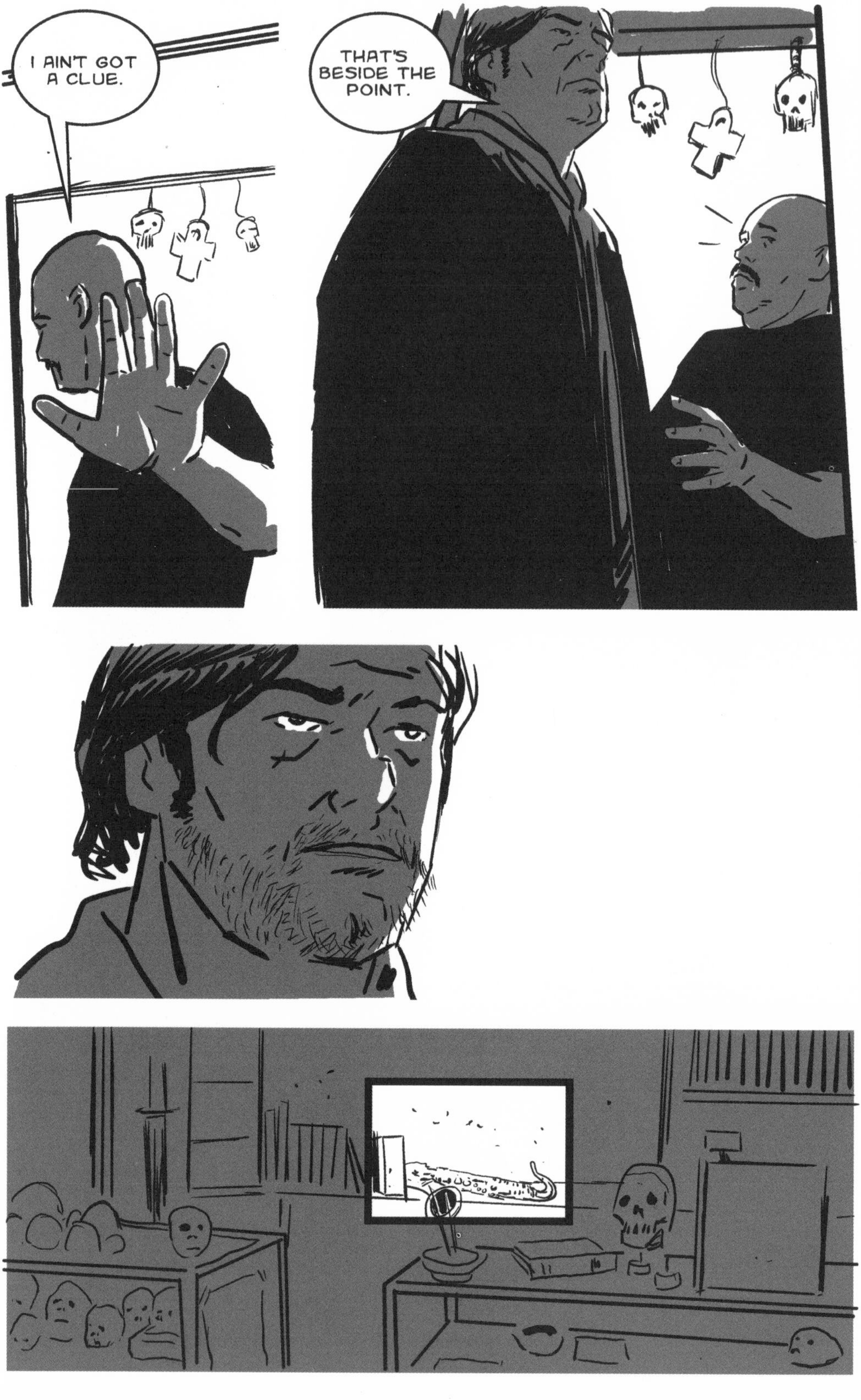
I AIN'T GOT A CLUE.
THAT'S BESIDE THE POINT.

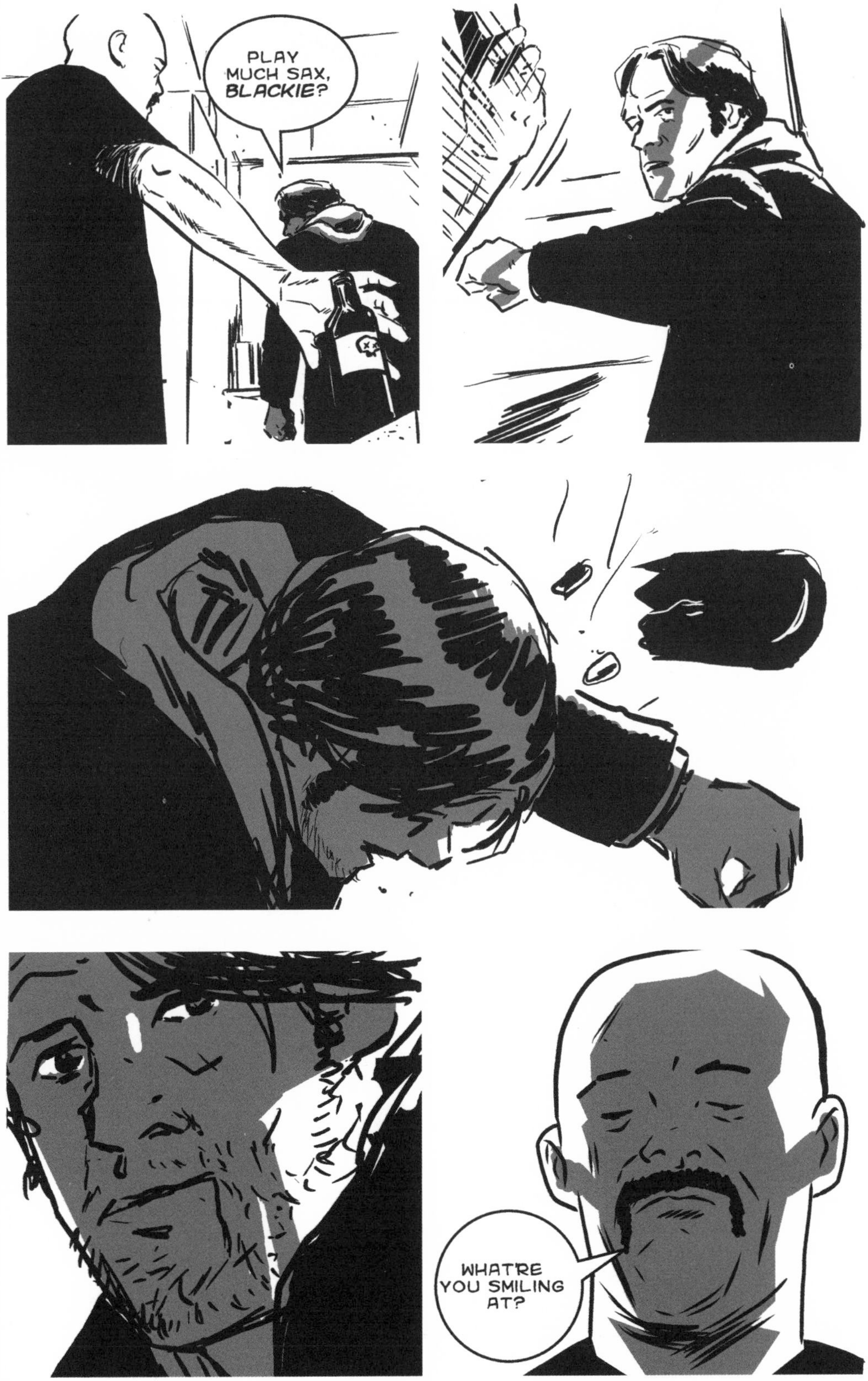
PLAY MUCH SAX, BLACKIE?
WHAT'RE YOU SMILING AT?

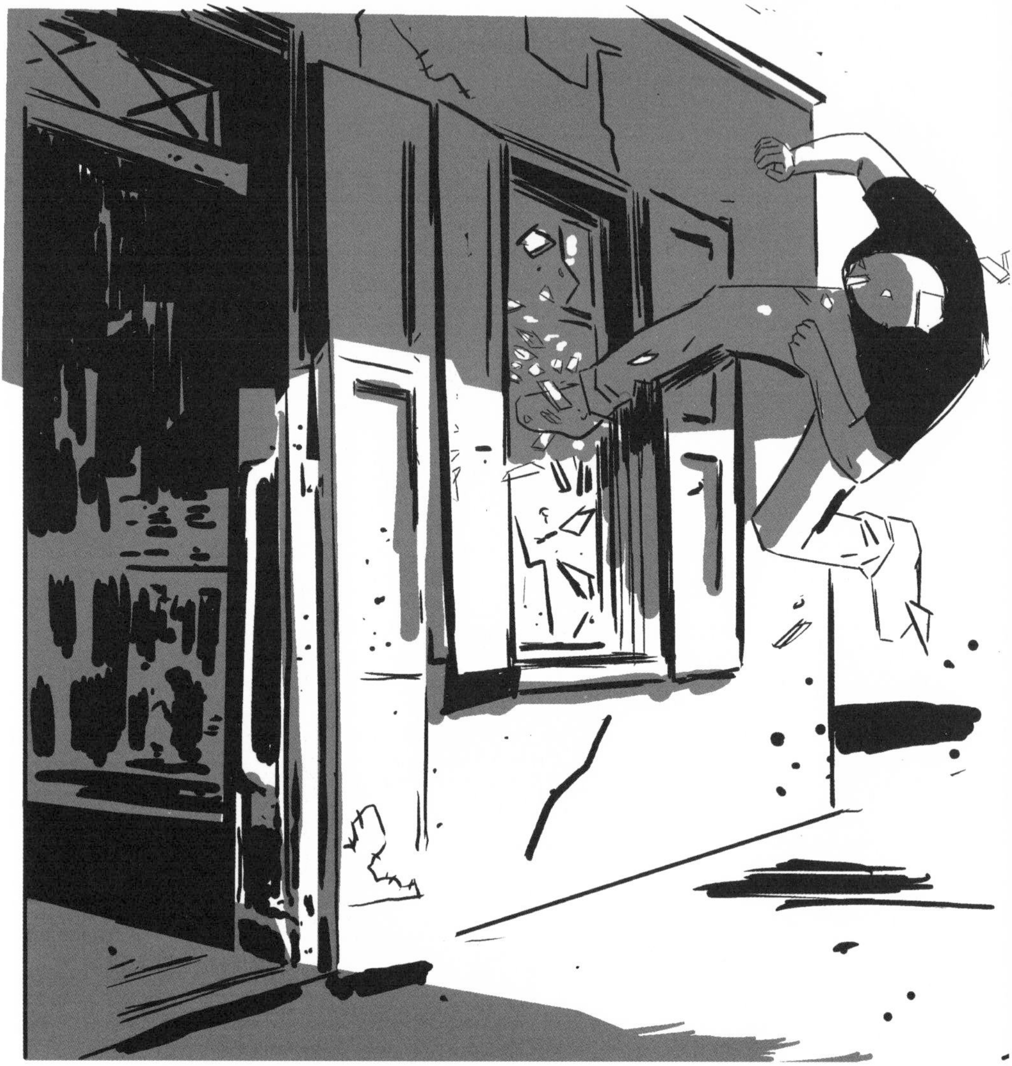

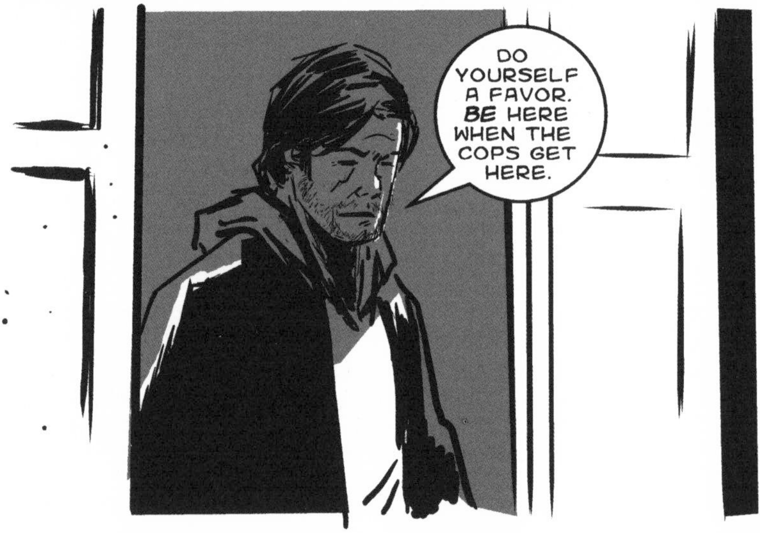
DO YOURSELF A FAVOR. BE HERE WHEN THE COPS GET HERE.

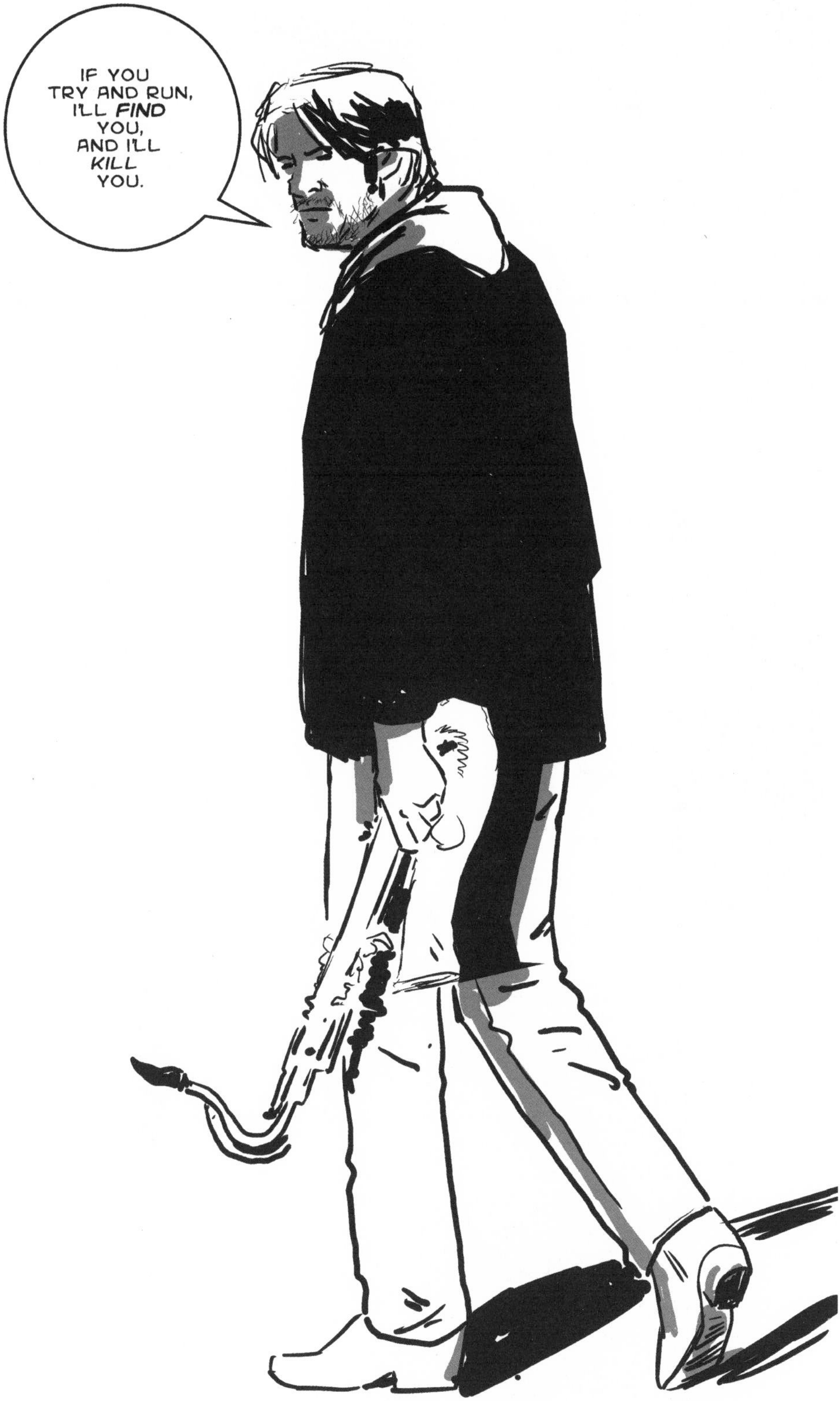
IF YOU TRY AND RUN, I'LL *FIND* YOU, AND I'LL *KILL* YOU.

CHAPTER SEVEN

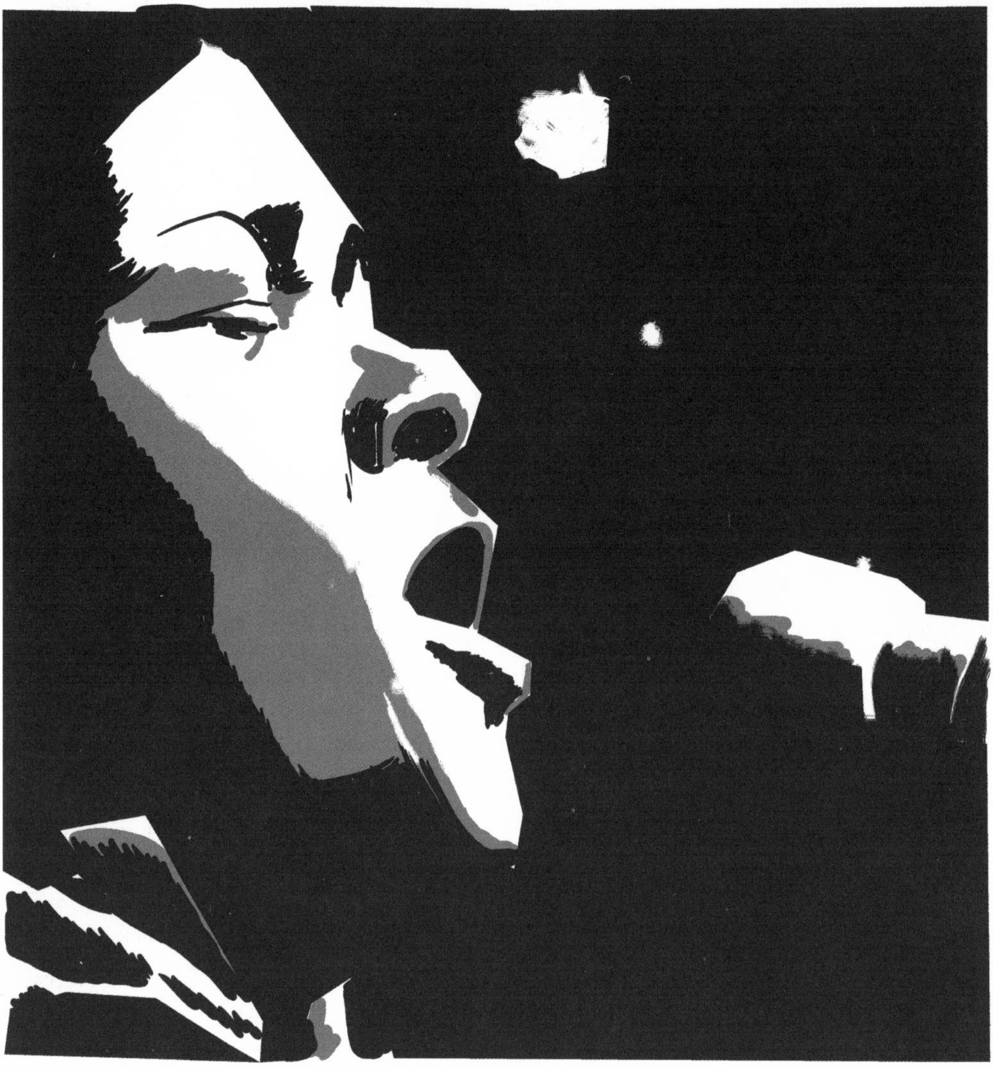

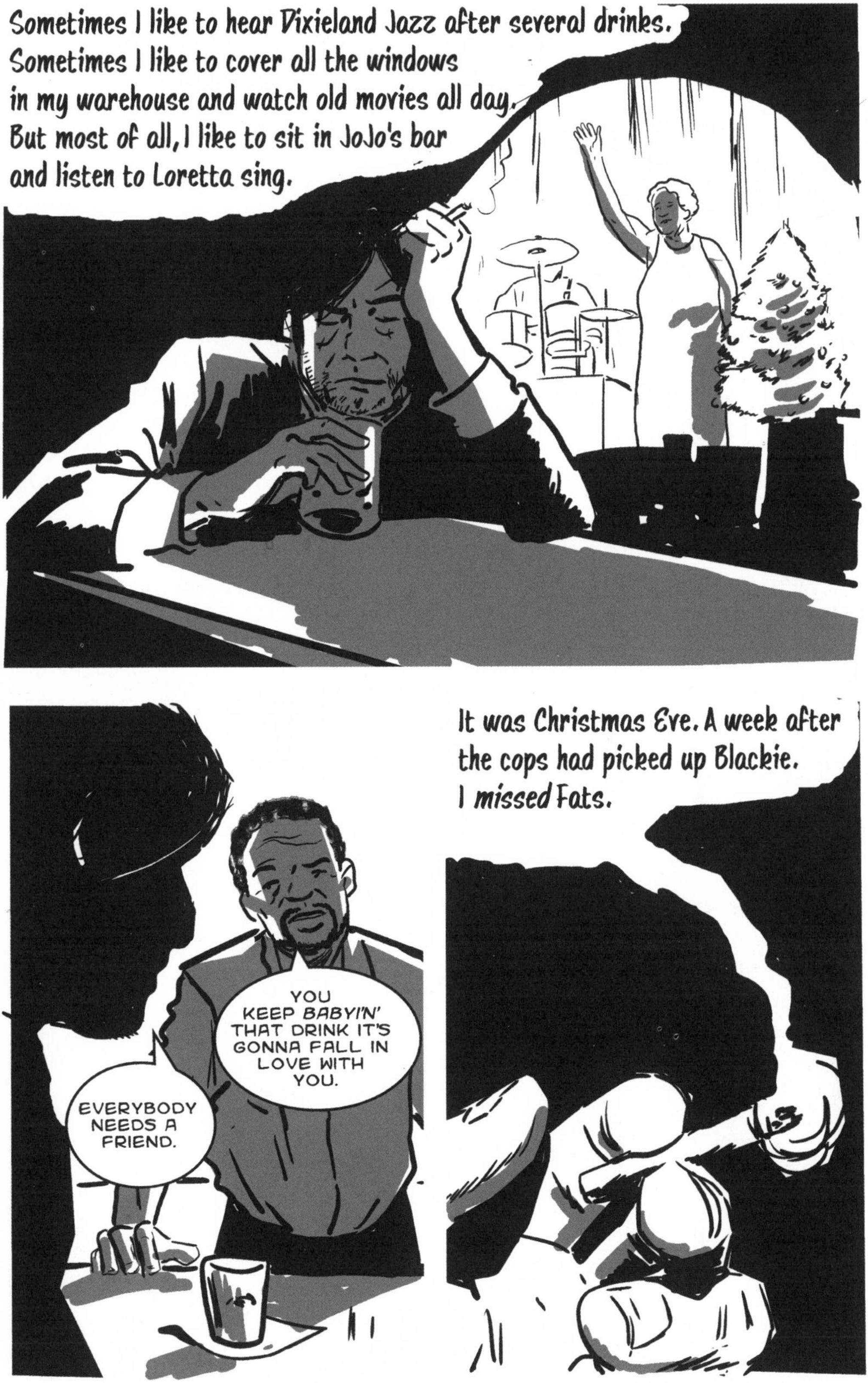
Sometimes I like to hear Dixieland Jazz after several drinks. Sometimes I like to cover all the windows in my warehouse and watch old movies all day. But most of all, I like to sit in JoJo's bar and listen to Loretta sing.
YOU KEEP *BABYIN'* THAT DRINK IT'S GONNA FALL IN LOVE WITH YOU.
EVERYBODY NEEDS A FRIEND.
It was Christmas Eve. A week after the cops had picked up Blackie.
I *missed* Fats.

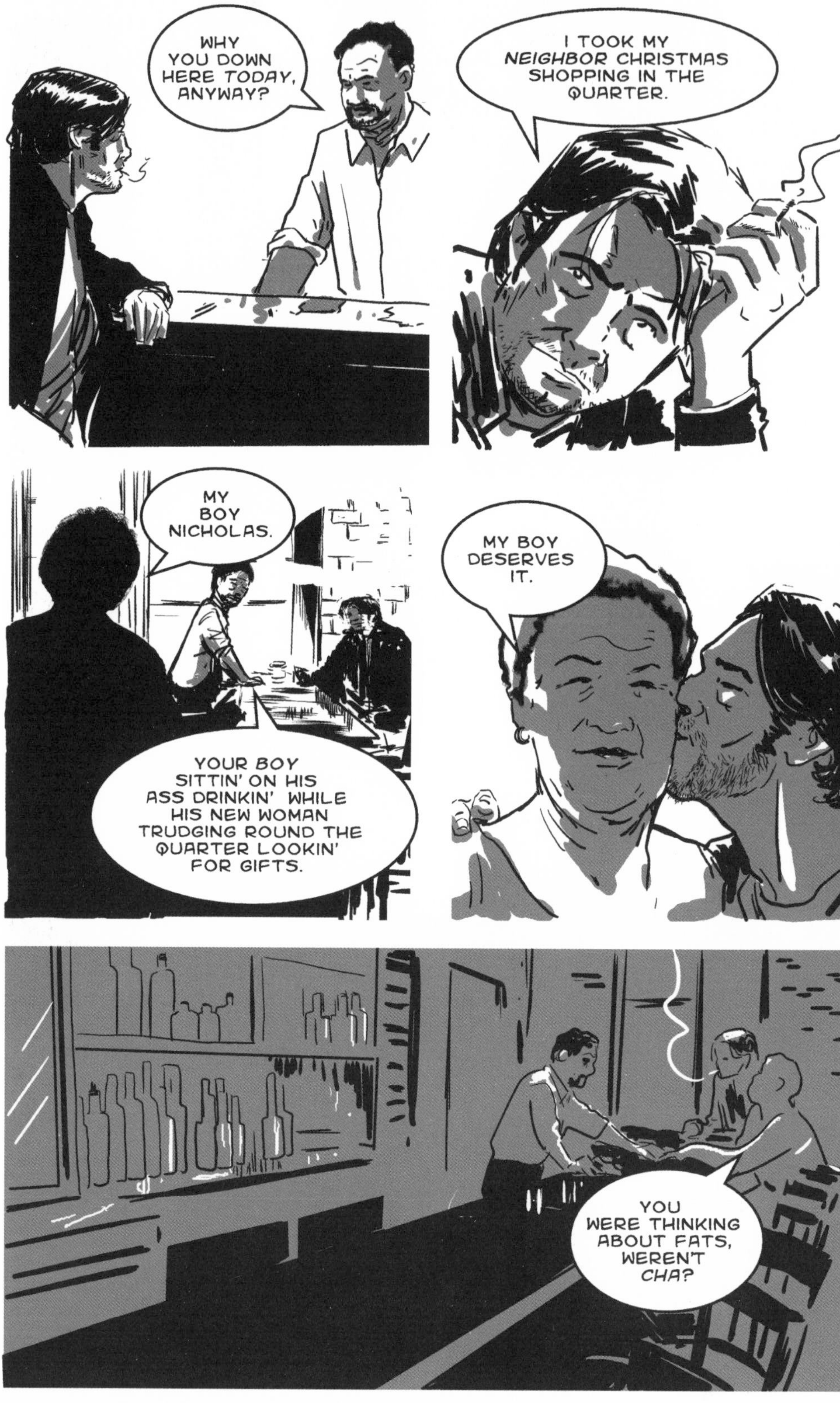
WHY YOU DOWN HERE TODAY, ANYWAY?
I TOOK MY NEIGHBOR CHRISTMAS SHOPPING IN THE QUARTER.
MY BOY NICHOLAS.
YOUR BOY SITTIN' ON HIS ASS DRINKIN' WHILE HIS NEW WOMAN TRUDGING ROUND THE QUARTER LOOKIN' FOR GIFTS.
MY BOY DESERVES IT.
YOU WERE THINKING ABOUT FATS, WEREN'T CHA?

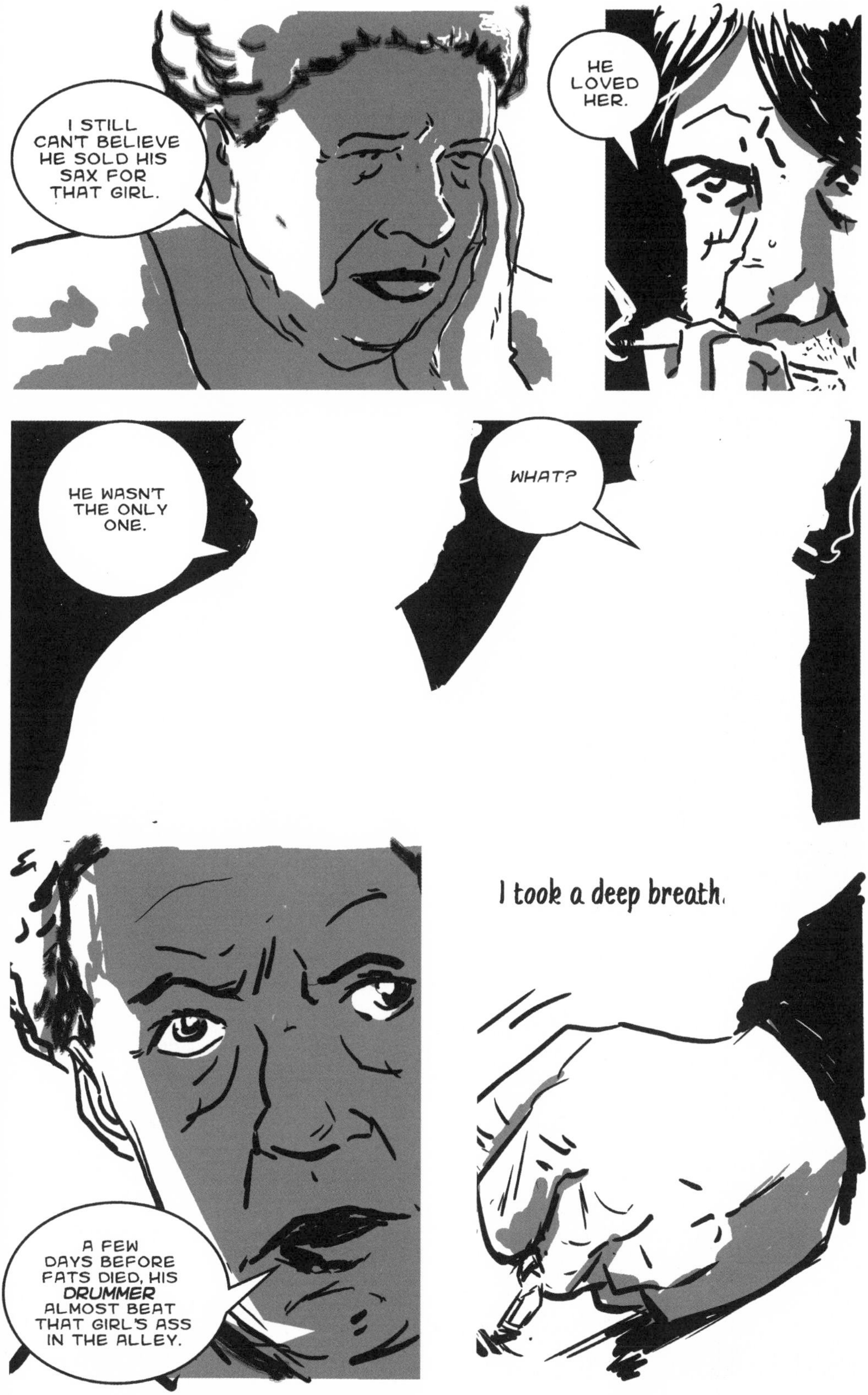
I STILL CAN'T BELIEVE HE SOLD HIS SAX FOR THAT GIRL.
HE LOVED HER.
HE WASN'T THE ONLY ONE.
WHAT?
A FEW DAYS BEFORE FATS DIED, HIS DRUMMER ALMOST BEAT THAT GIRL'S ASS IN THE ALLEY.
I took a deep breath.

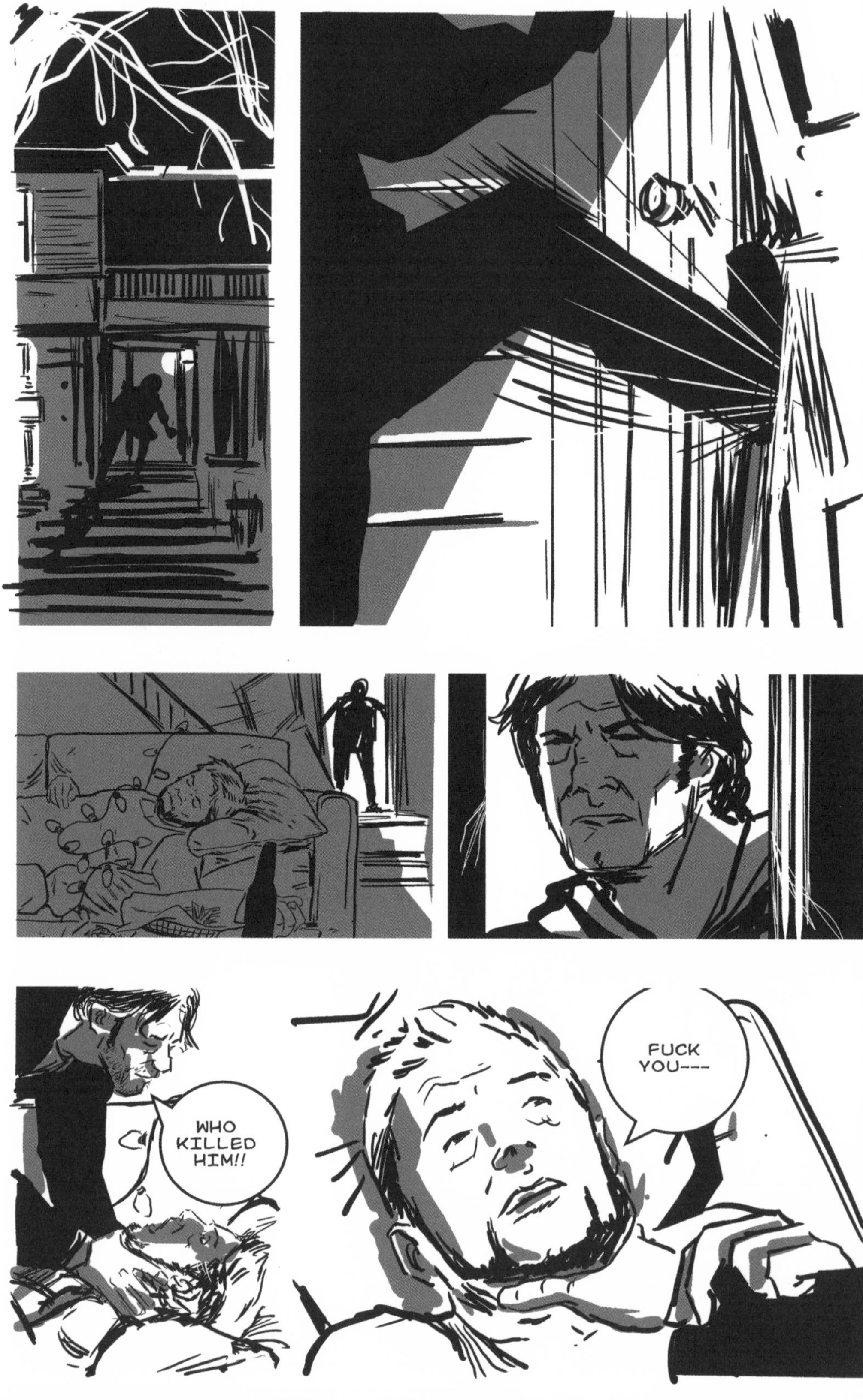
WHO KILLED HIM!!
FUCK YOU---

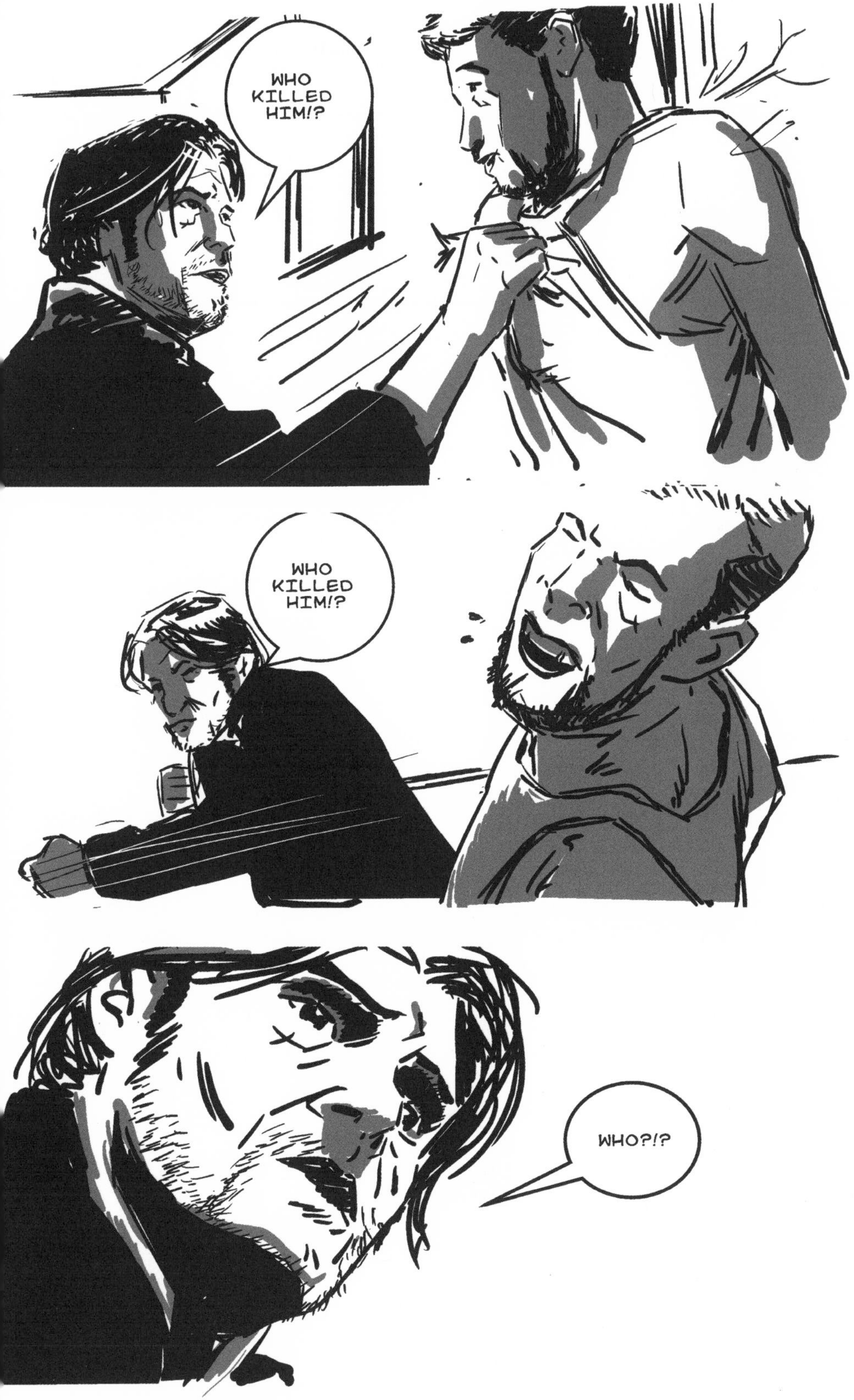
WHO KILLED HIM!?
WHO KILLED HIM!?
WHO?!?

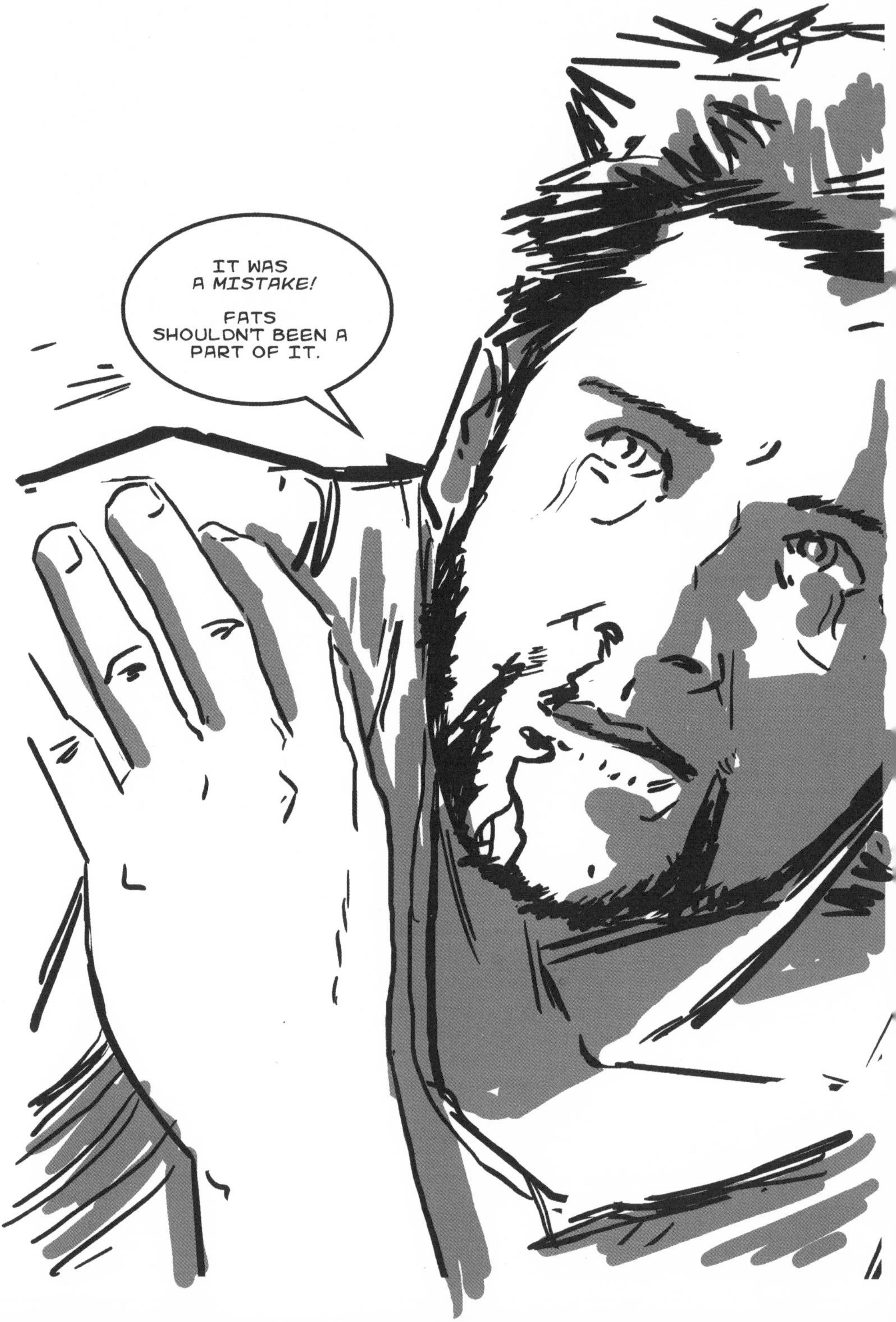
IT WAS A *MISTAKE!*
FATS SHOULDN'T BEEN A PART OF IT.

CHAPTER EIGHT

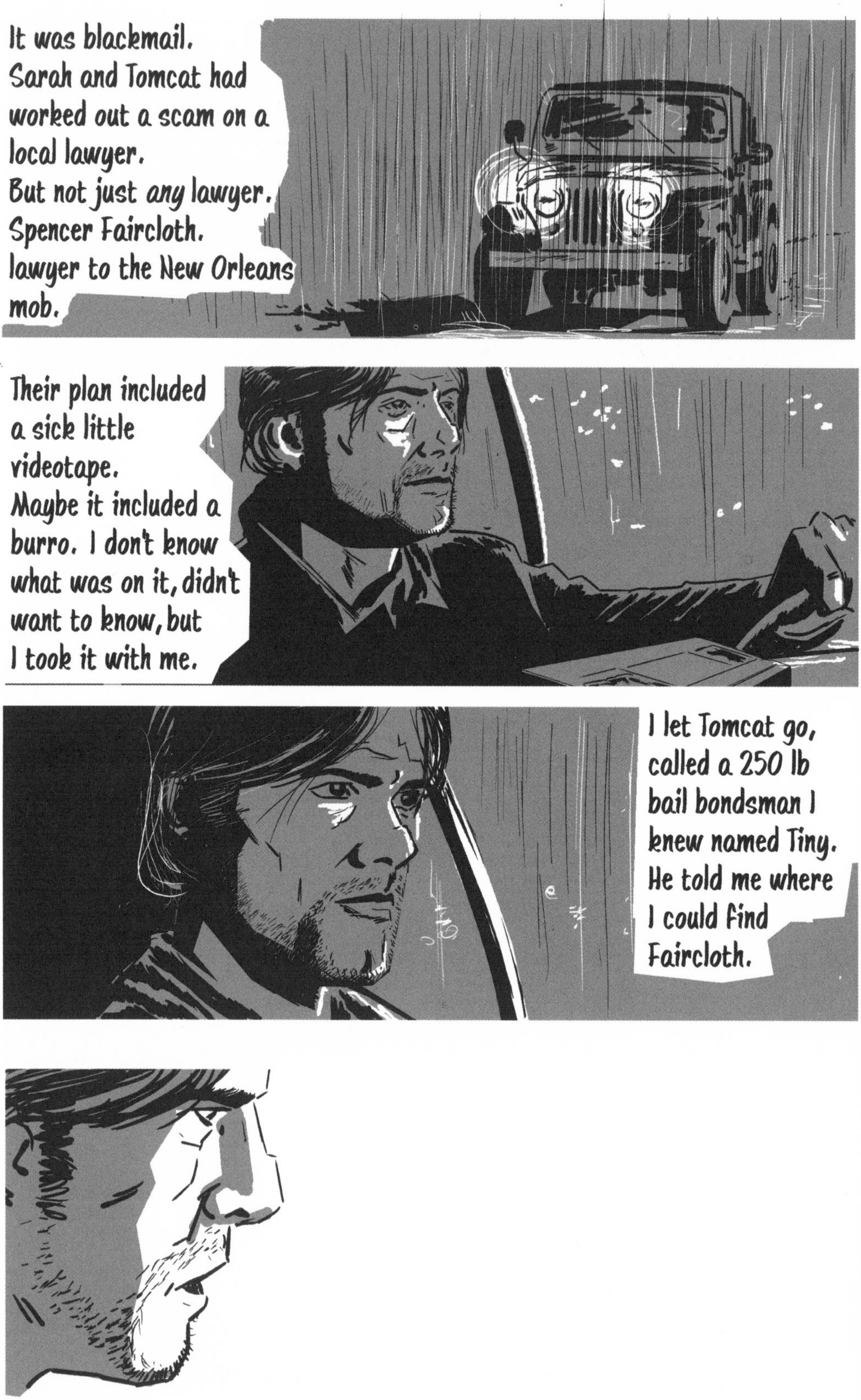
It was blackmail. Sarah and Tomcat had worked out a scam on a local lawyer. But not just *any* lawyer. Spencer Faircloth. lawyer to the New Orleans mob.
Their plan included a sick little videotape. Maybe it included a burro. I don't know what was on it, didn't want to know, but I took it with me.
I let Tomcat go, called a 250 lb bail bondsman I knew named Tiny. He told me where I could find Faircloth.

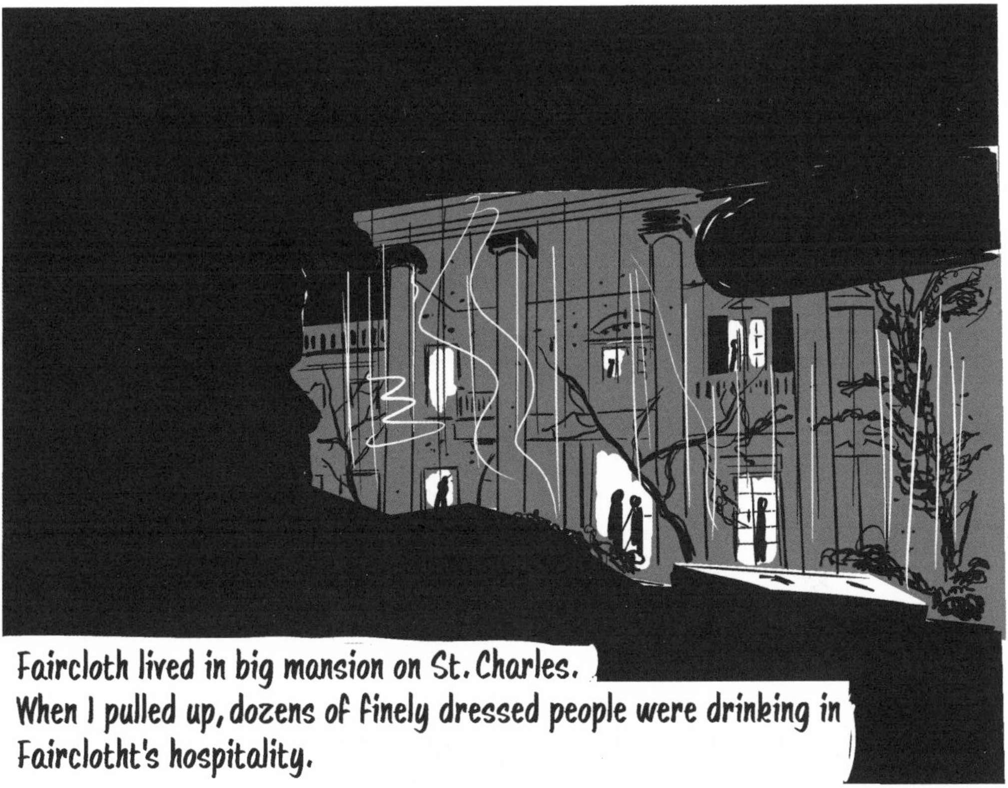
Faircloth lived in big mansion on St. Charles.
When I pulled up, dozens of finely dressed people were drinking in Fairclotht's hospitality.

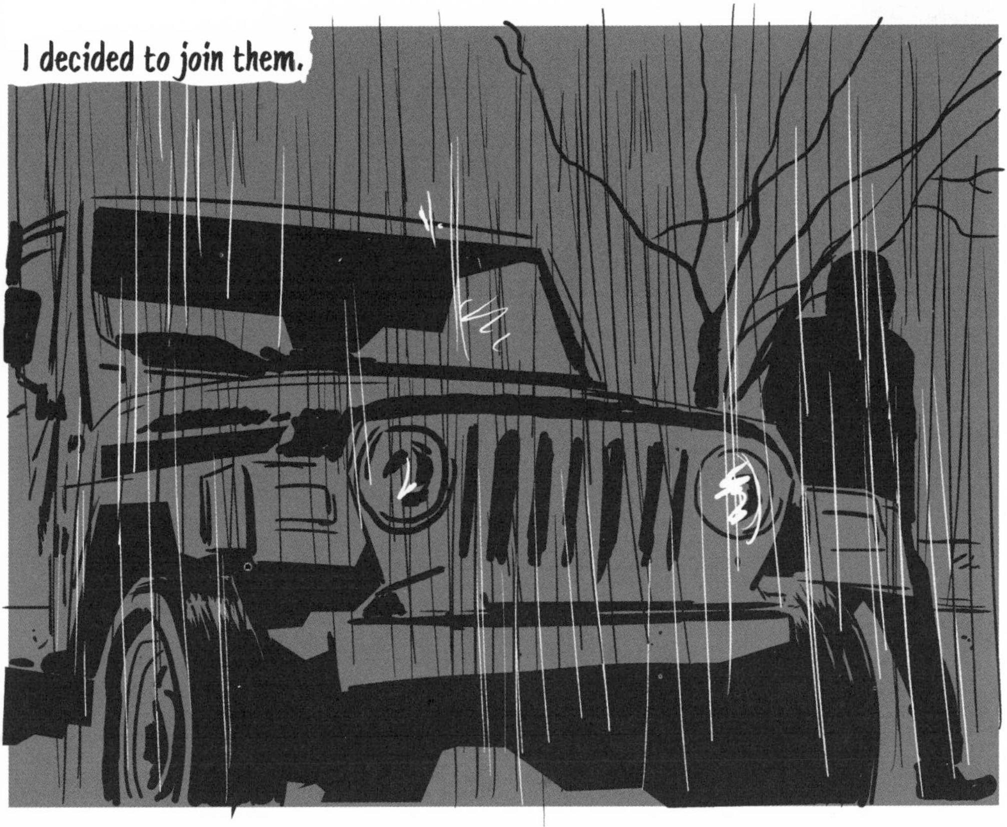
I decided to join them.

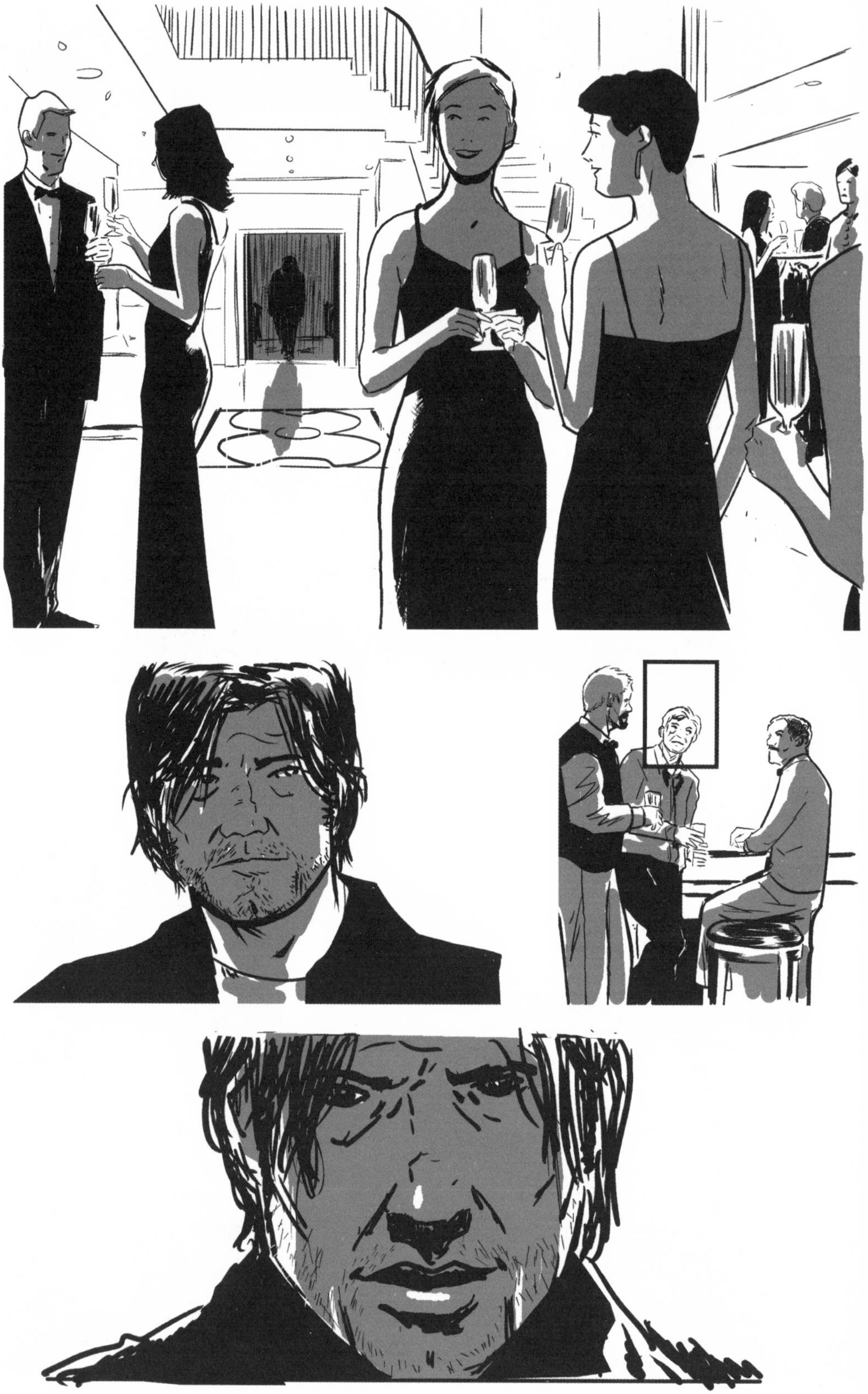

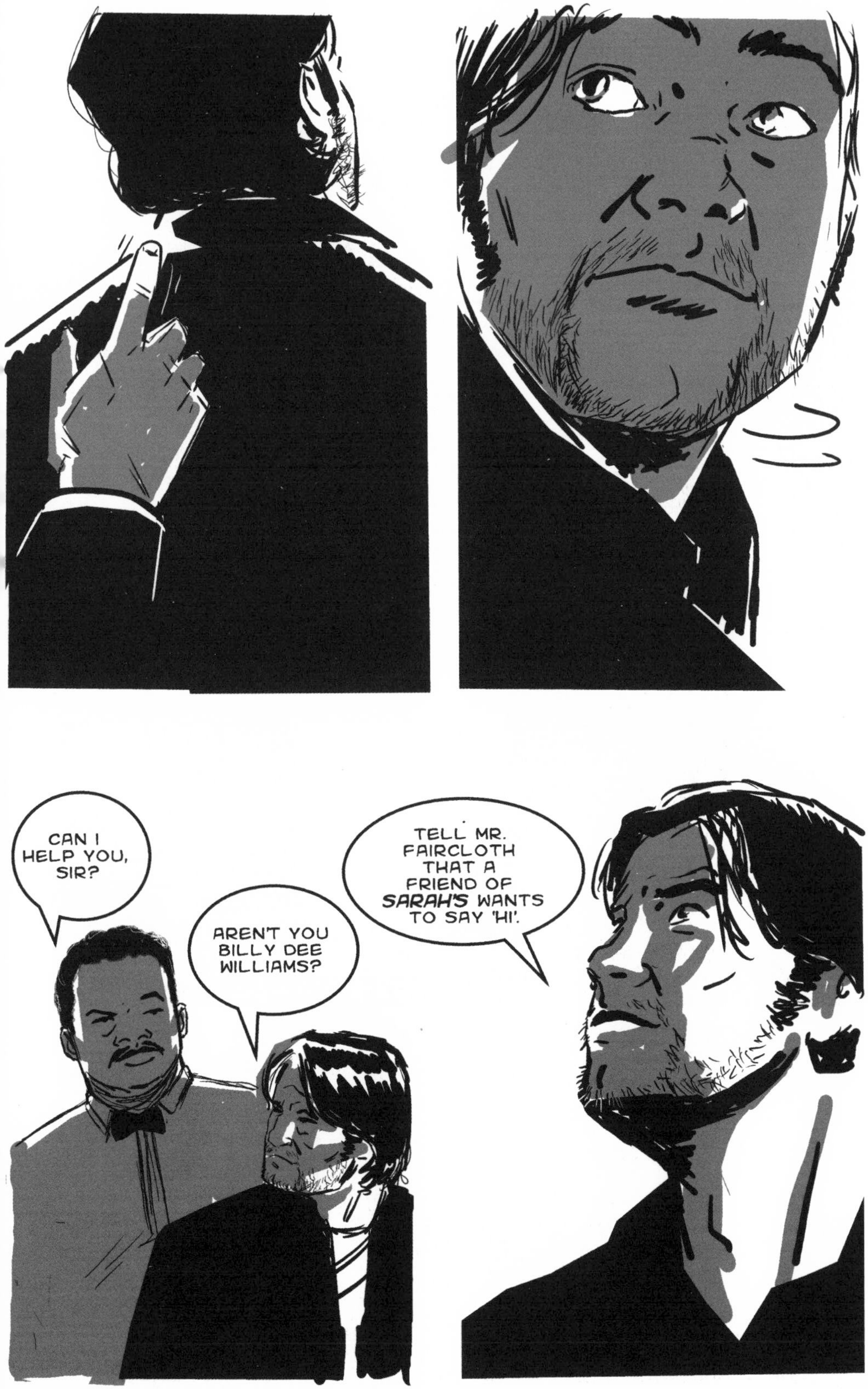
CAN I HELP YOU, SIR?
AREN'T YOU BILLY DEE WILLIAMS?
TELL MR. FAIRCLOTH THAT A FRIEND OF *SARAH'S* WANTS TO SAY 'HI'.

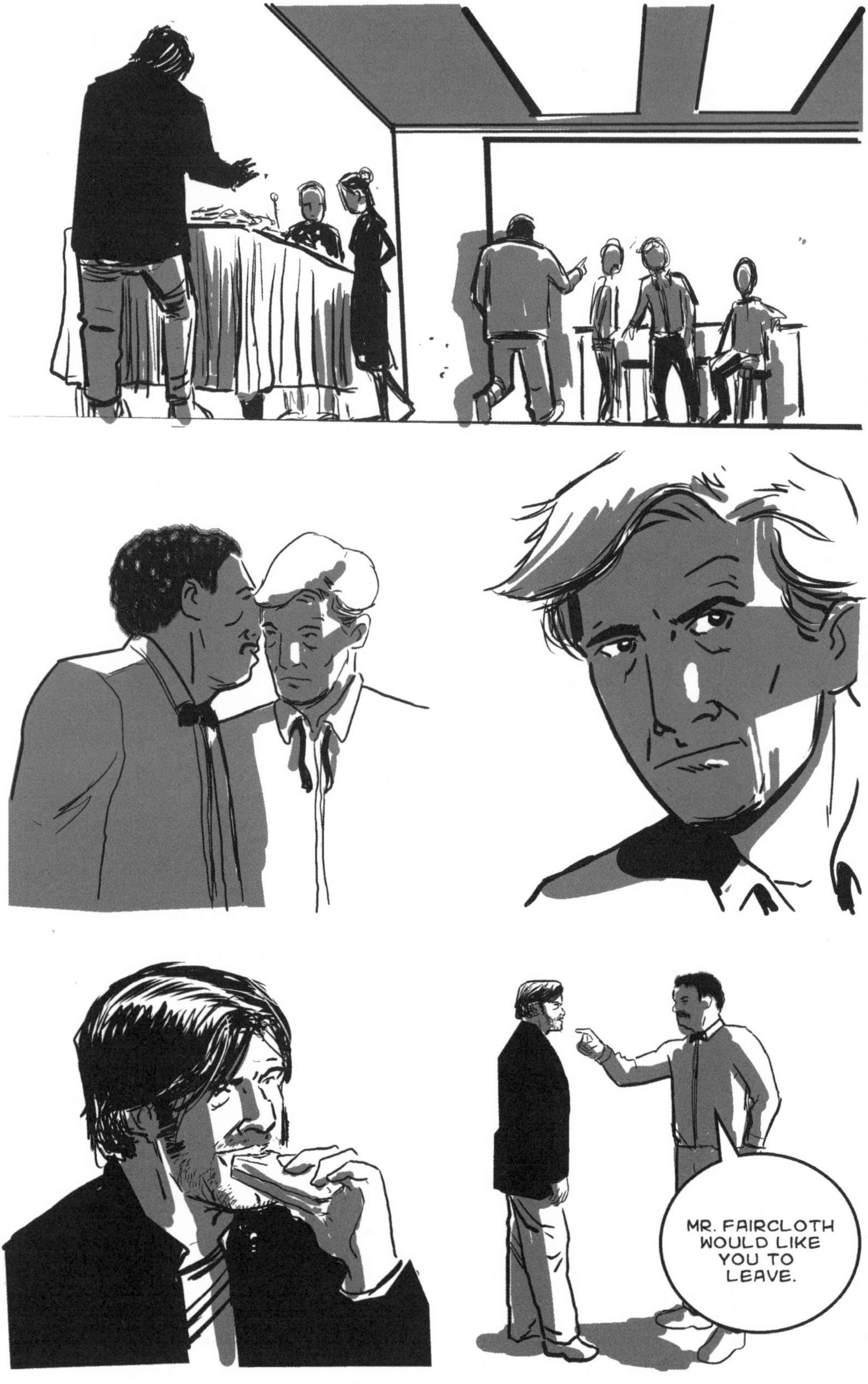
MR. FAIRCLOTH WOULD LIKE YOU TO LEAVE.

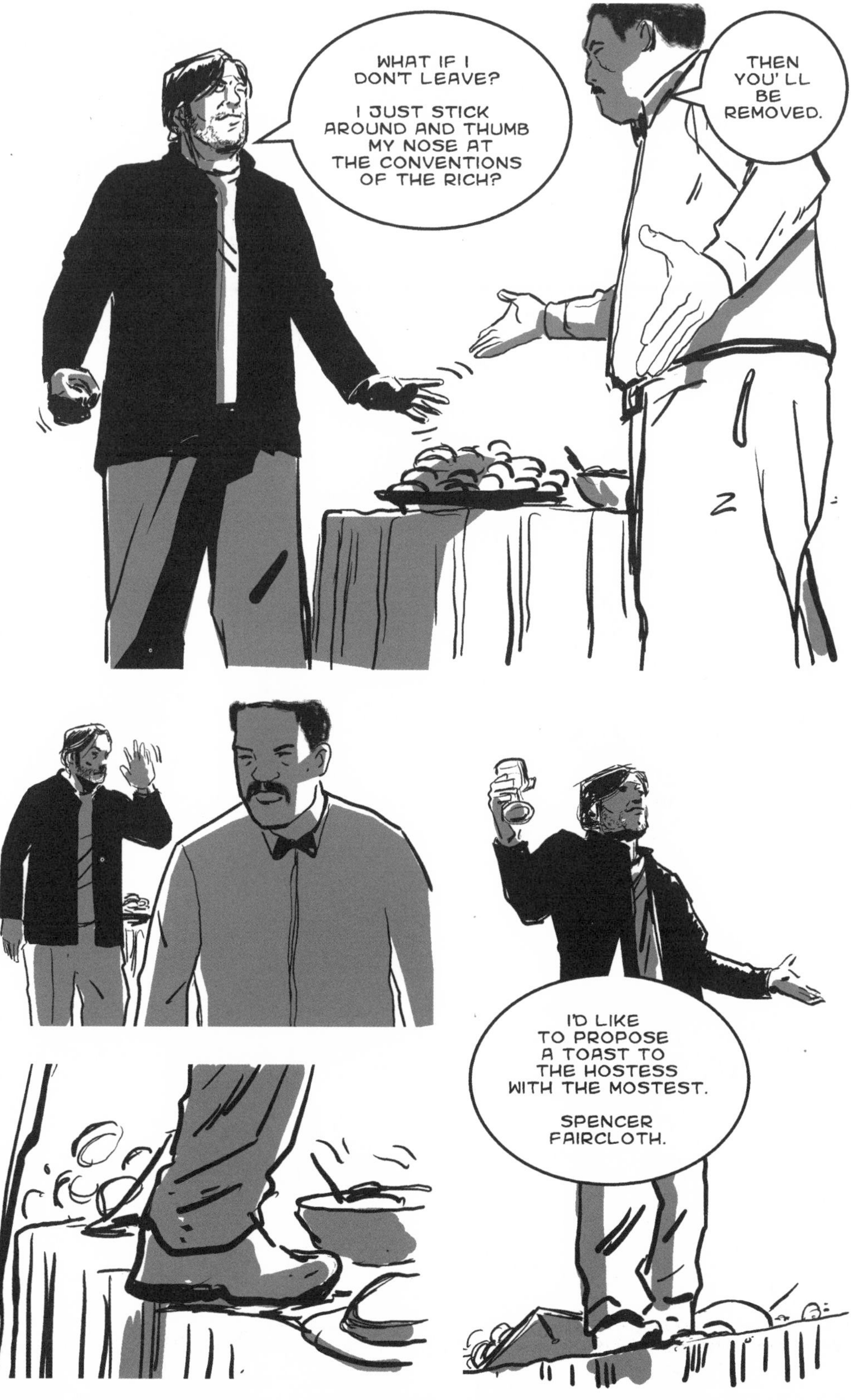
WHAT IF I DON'T LEAVE?
I JUST STICK AROUND AND THUMB MY NOSE AT THE CONVENTIONS OF THE RICH?
THEN YOU'LL BE REMOVED.
I'D LIKE TO PROPOSE A TOAST TO THE HOSTESS WITH THE MOSTEST.
SPENCER FAIRCLOTH.

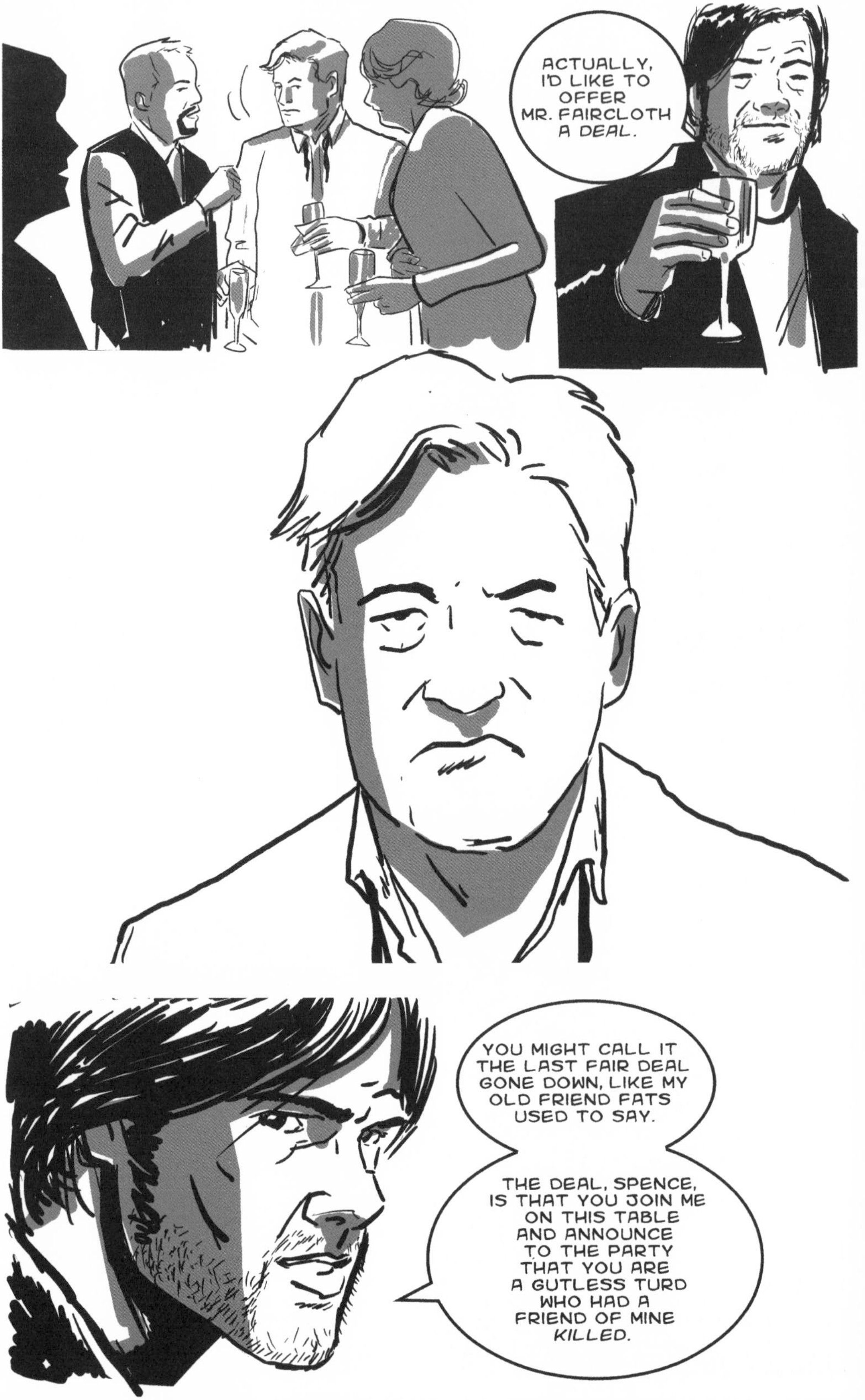
ACTUALLY, I'D LIKE TO OFFER MR. FAIRCLOTH A *DEAL*.
YOU MIGHT CALL IT THE LAST FAIR DEAL GONE DOWN, LIKE MY OLD FRIEND FATS USED TO SAY.
THE DEAL, SPENCE, IS THAT YOU JOIN ME ON THIS TABLE AND ANNOUNCE TO THE PARTY THAT YOU ARE A GUTLESS TURD WHO HAD A FRIEND OF MINE *KILLED*.

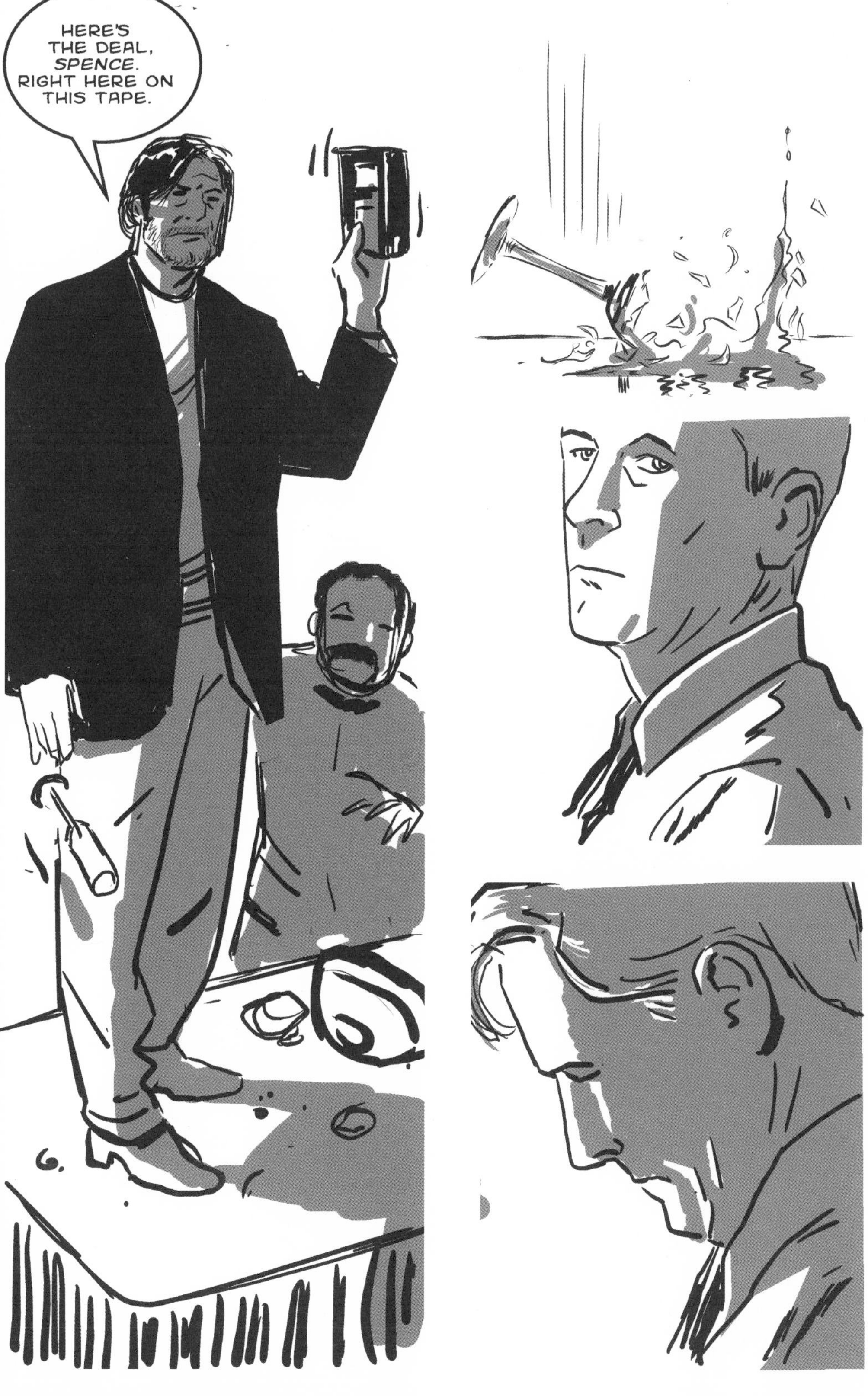
HERE'S THE DEAL, *SPENCE*. RIGHT HERE ON THIS TAPE.

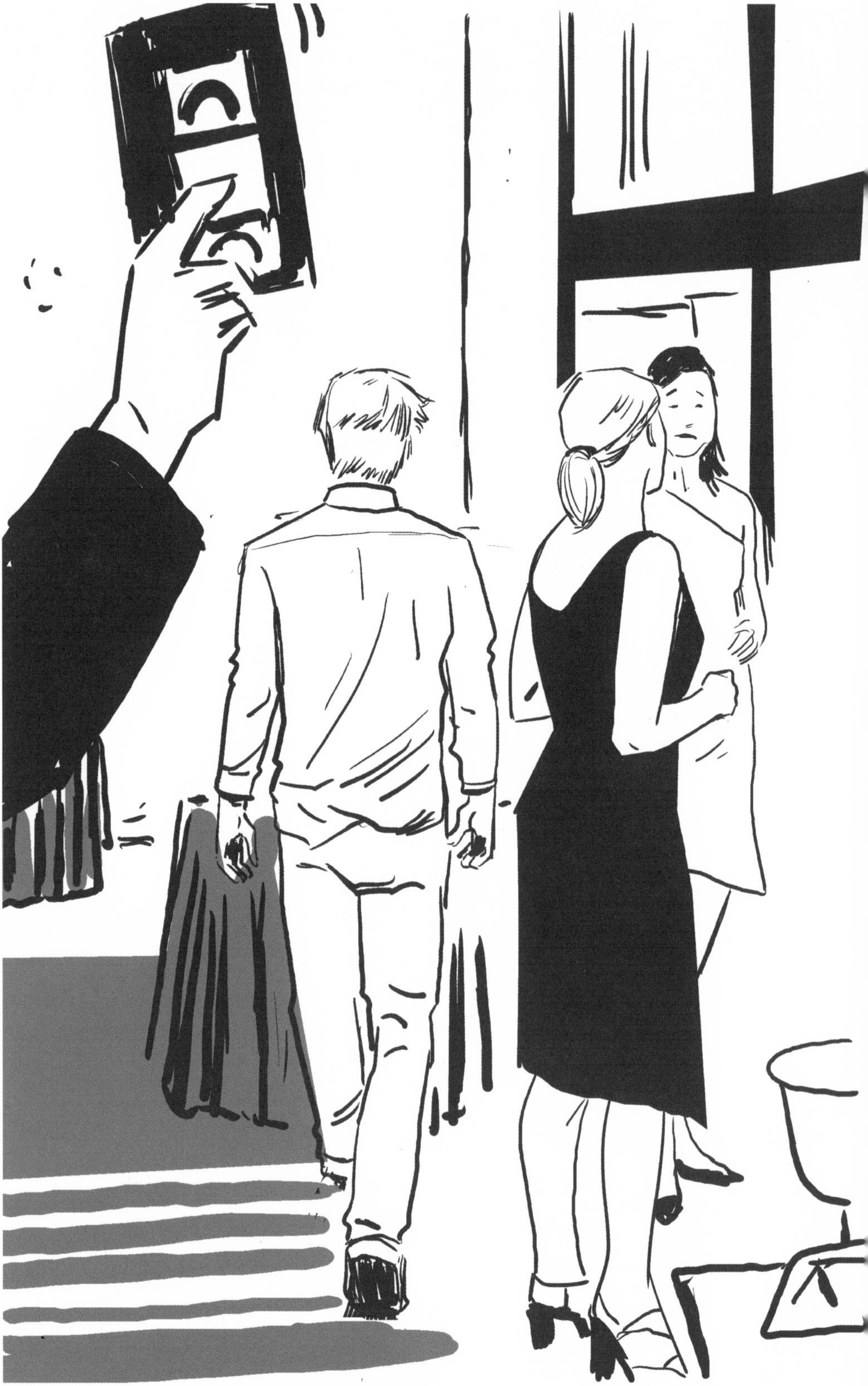

CHAPTER NINE

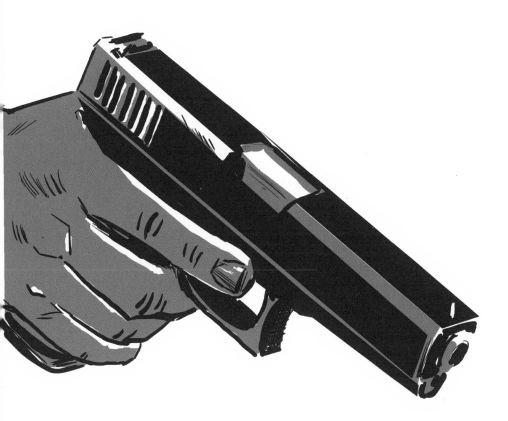

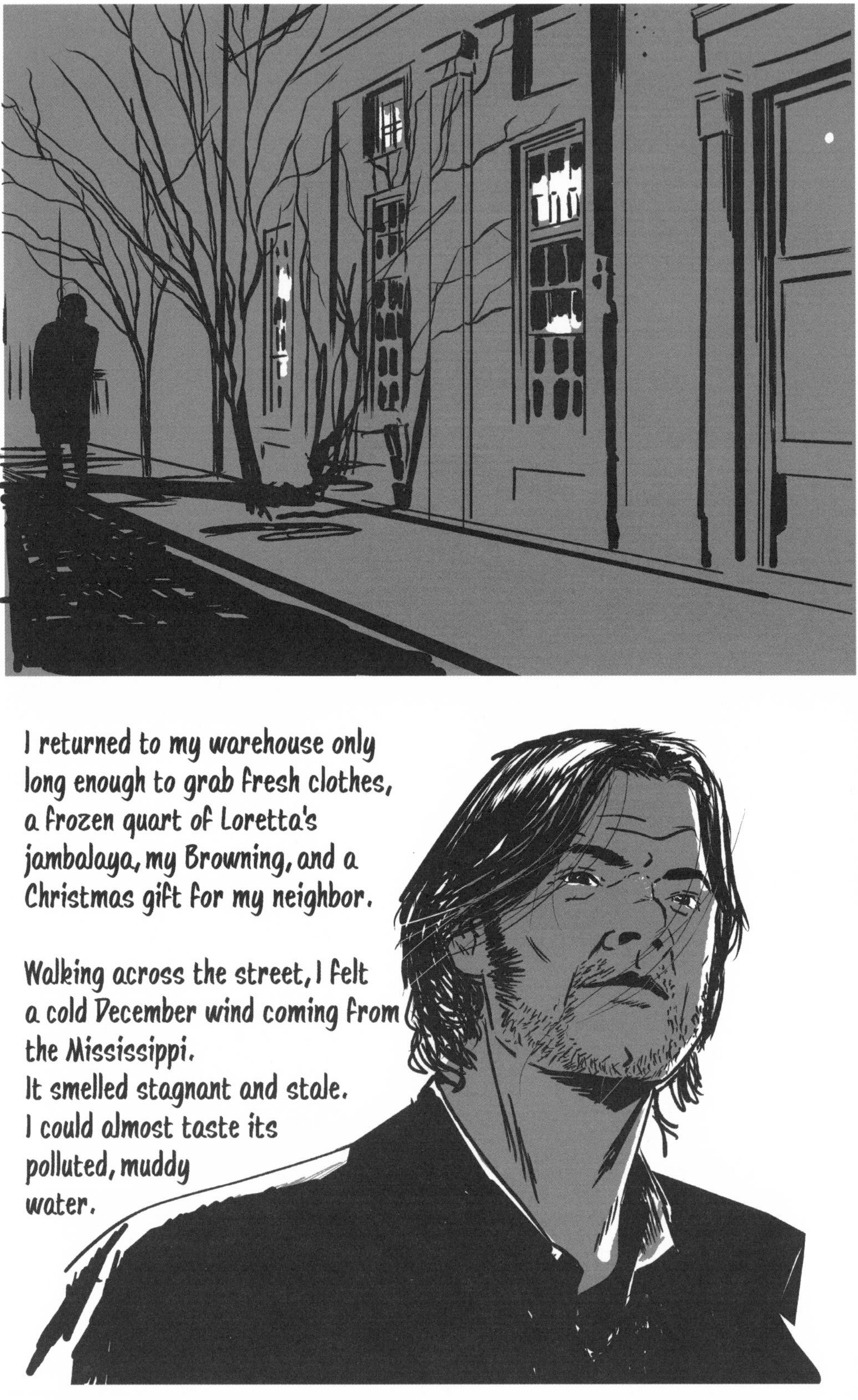
I returned to my warehouse only long enough to grab fresh clothes, a frozen quart of Loretta's jambalaya, my Browning, and a Christmas gift for my neighbor.
Walking across the street, I felt a cold December wind coming from the Mississippi.
It smelled stagnant and stale.
I could almost taste its polluted, muddy water.

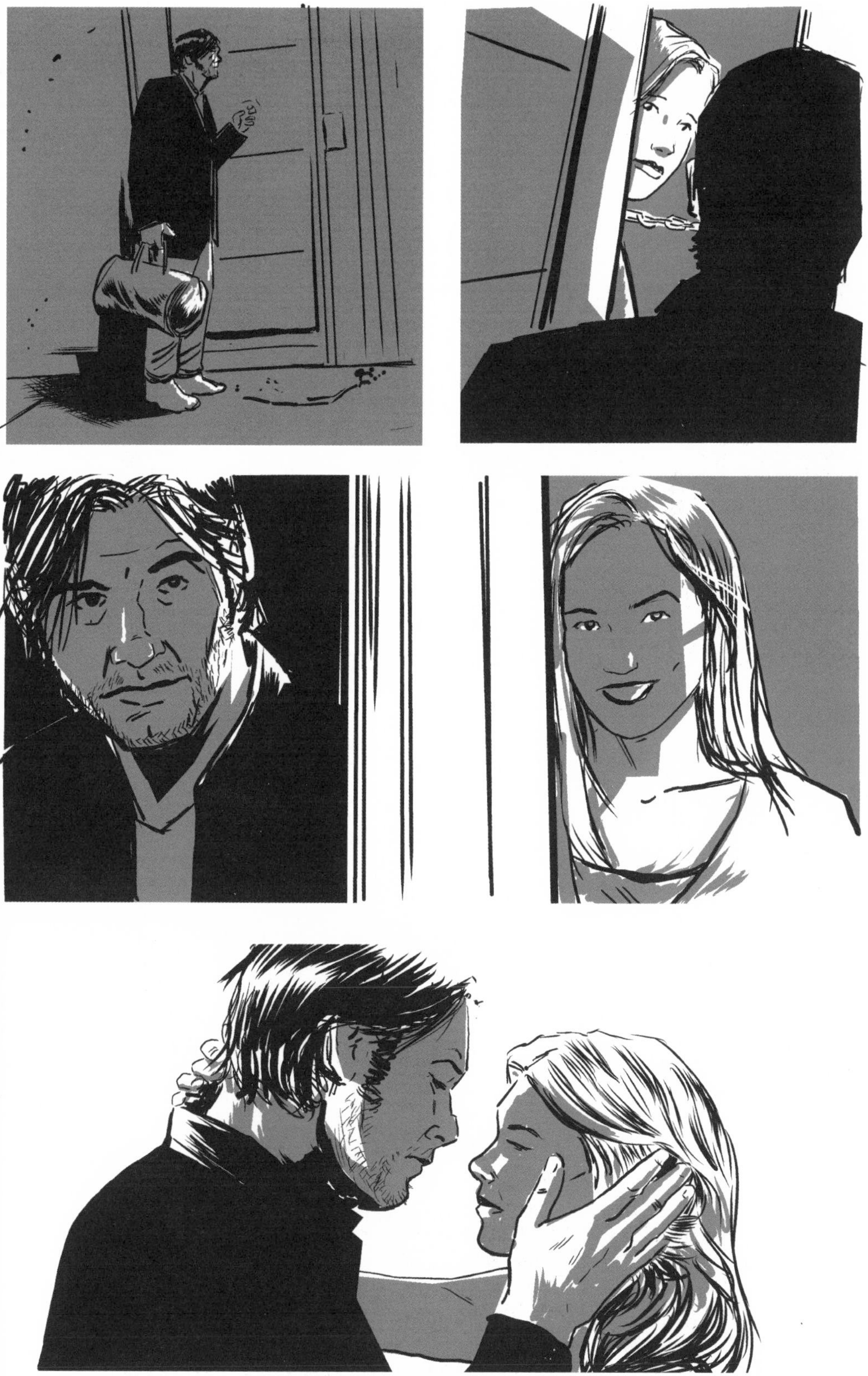

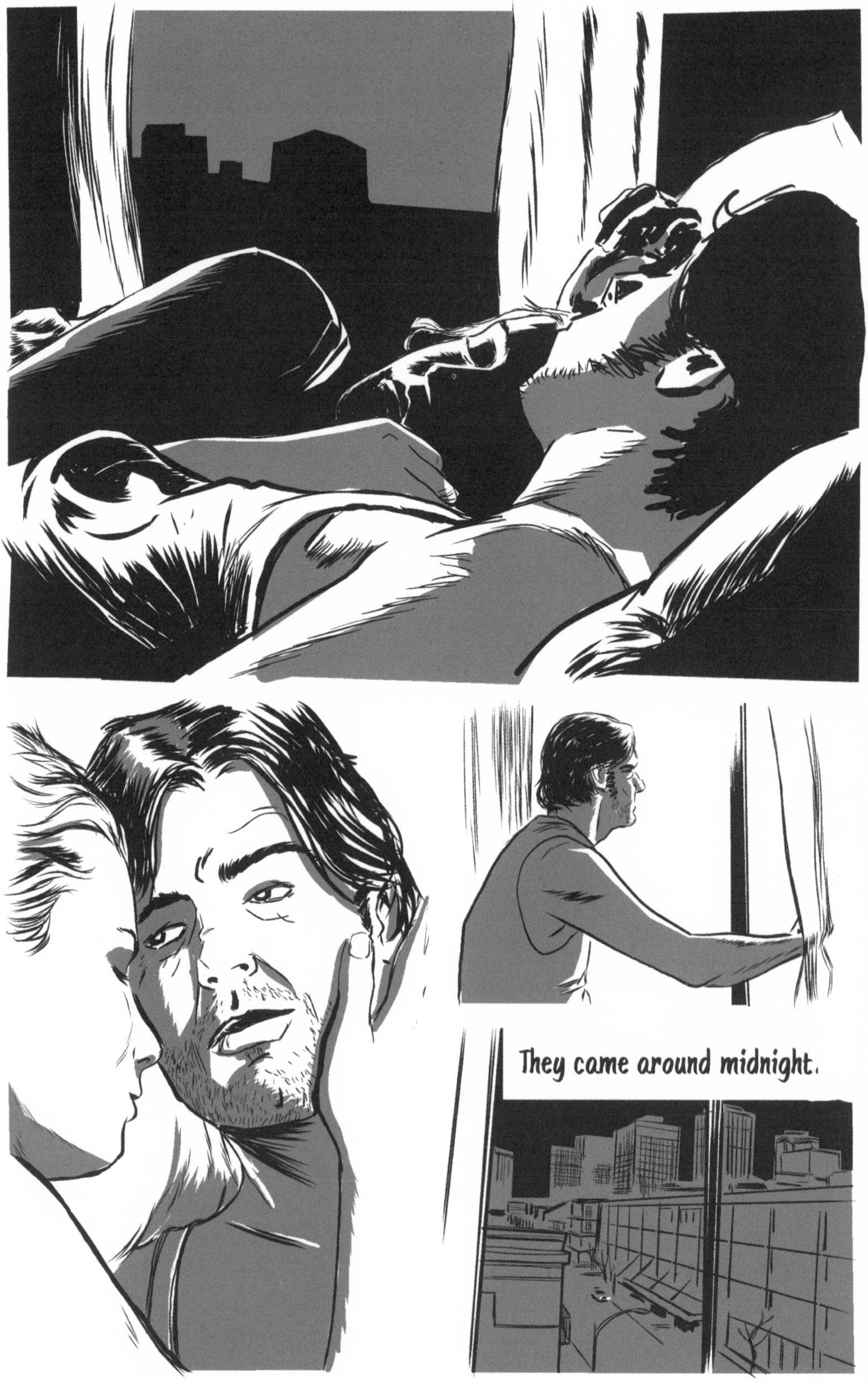
They came around midnight.

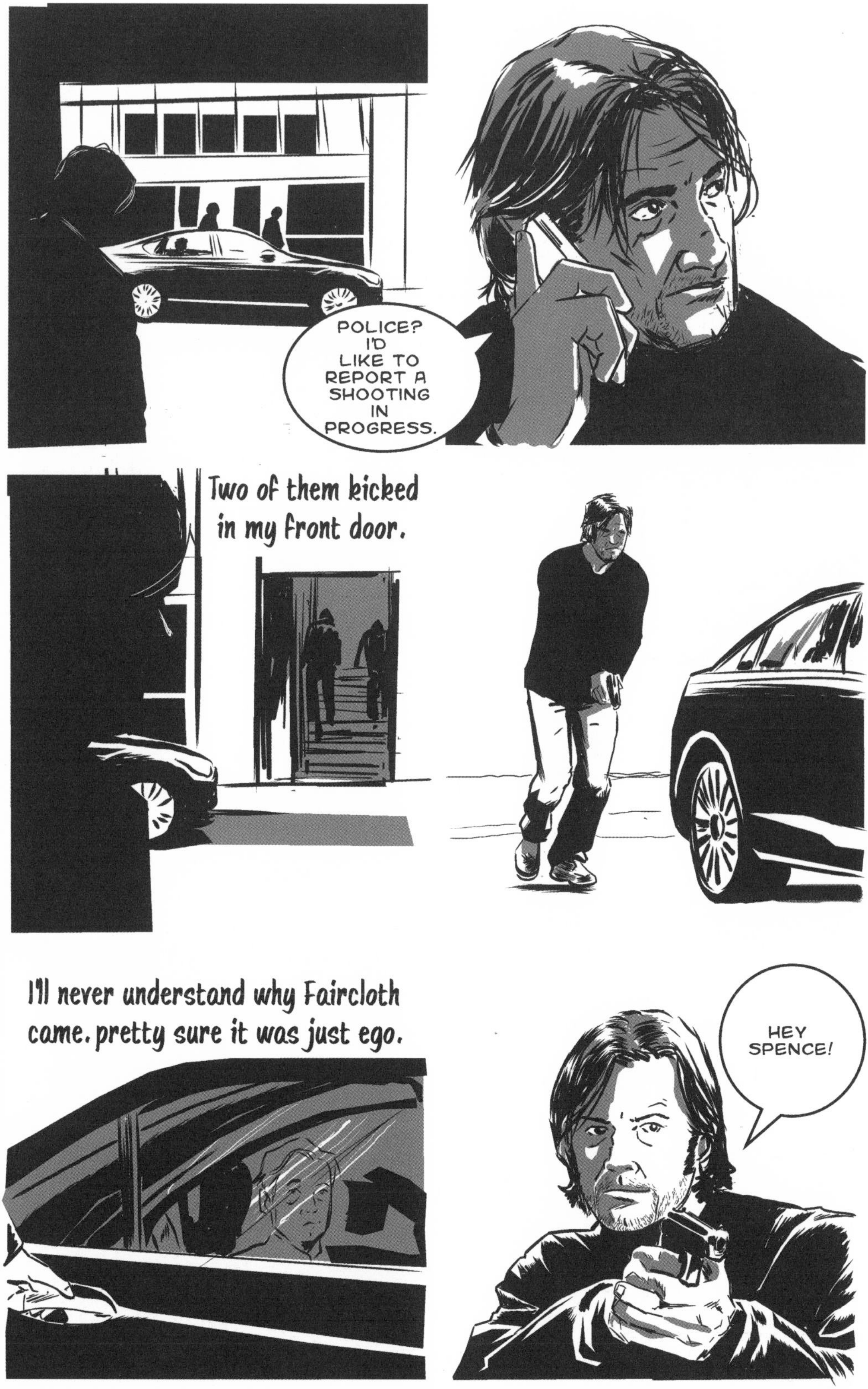
POLICE? I'D LIKE TO REPORT A SHOOTING IN PROGRESS.
Two of them kicked in my front door.
I'll never understand why Faircloth came. pretty sure it was just ego.
HEY SPENCE!

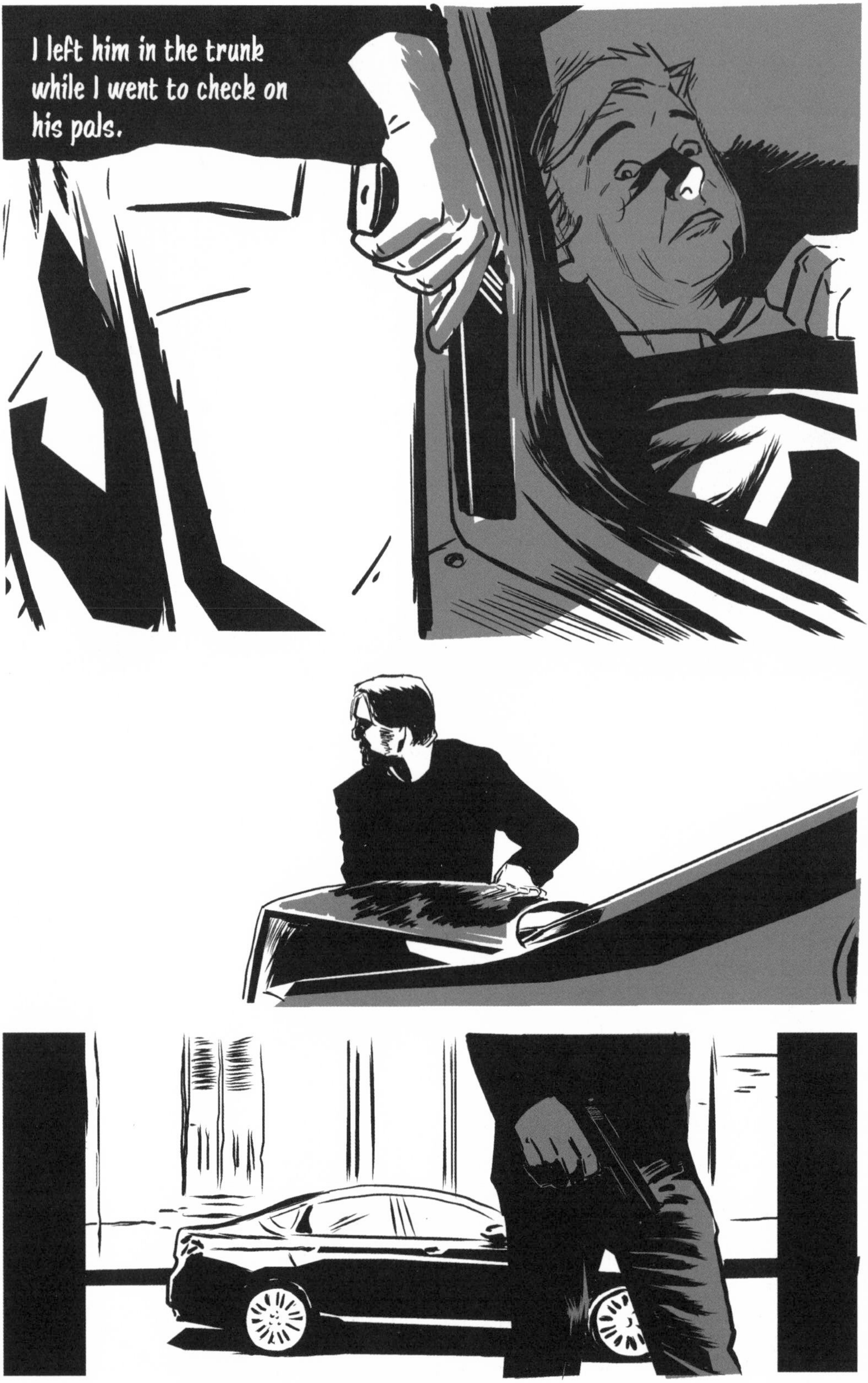
I left him in the trunk while I went to check on his pals.

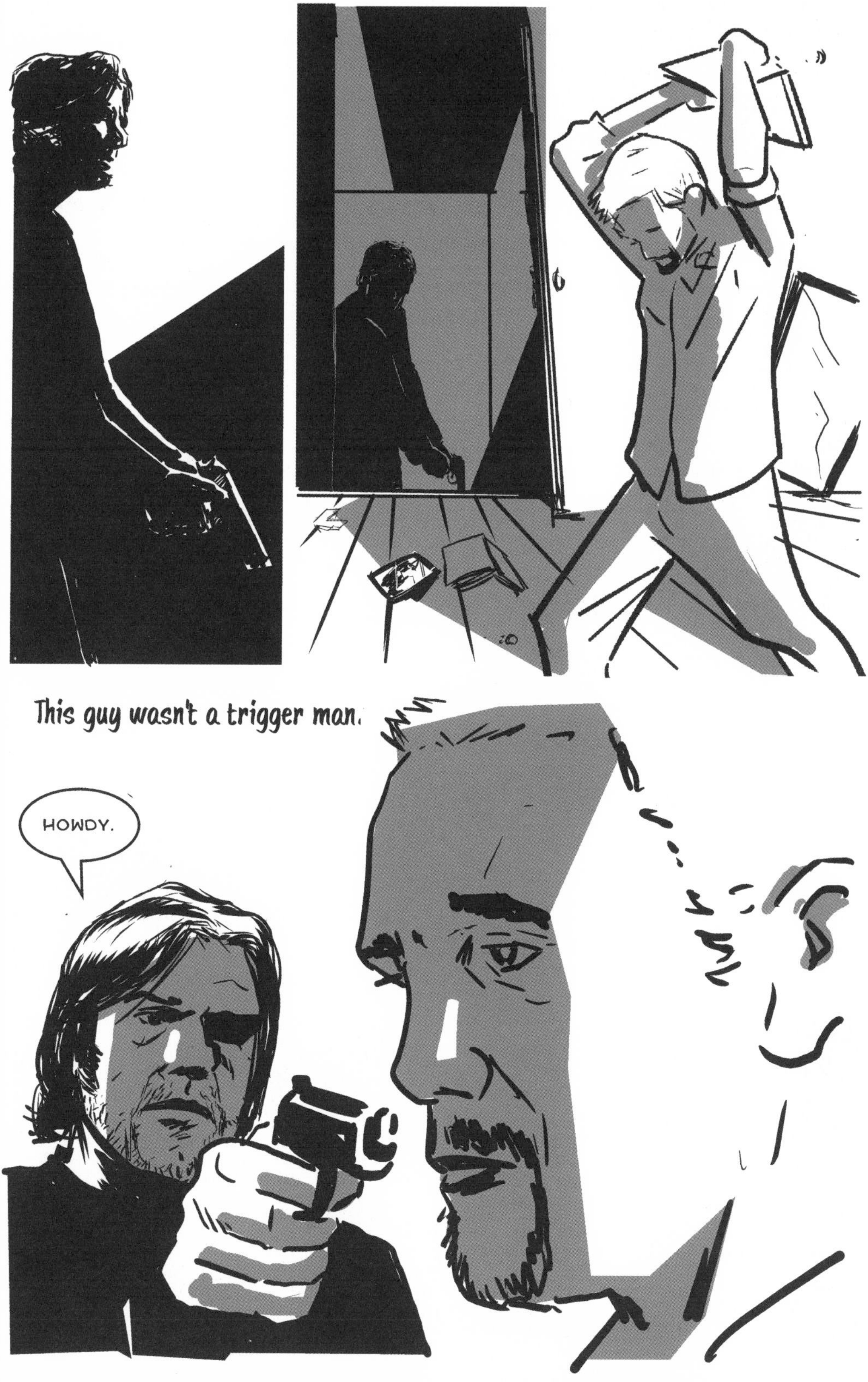
This guy wasn't a trigger man.
HOWDY.

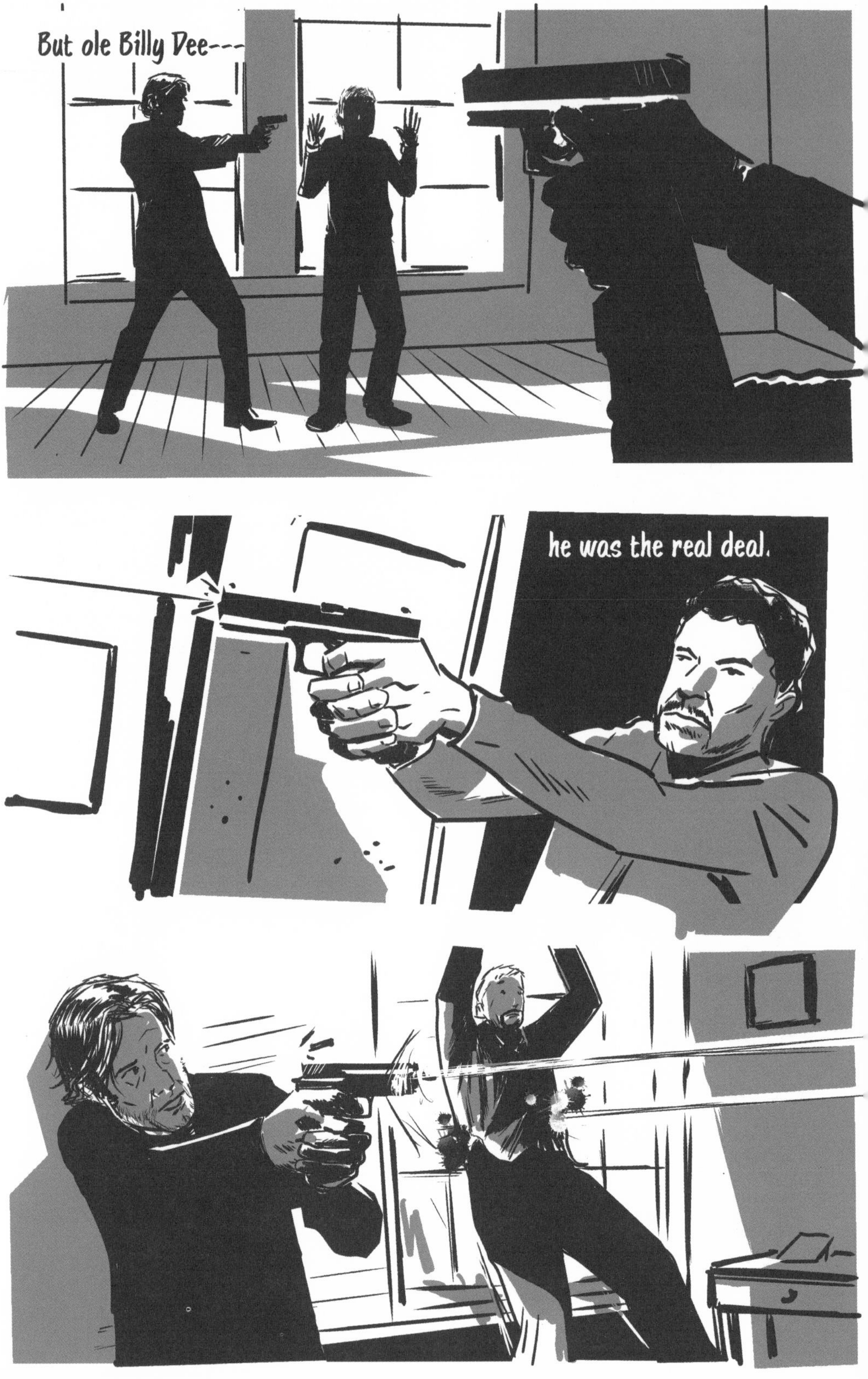
But ole Billy Dee---
he was the real deal.

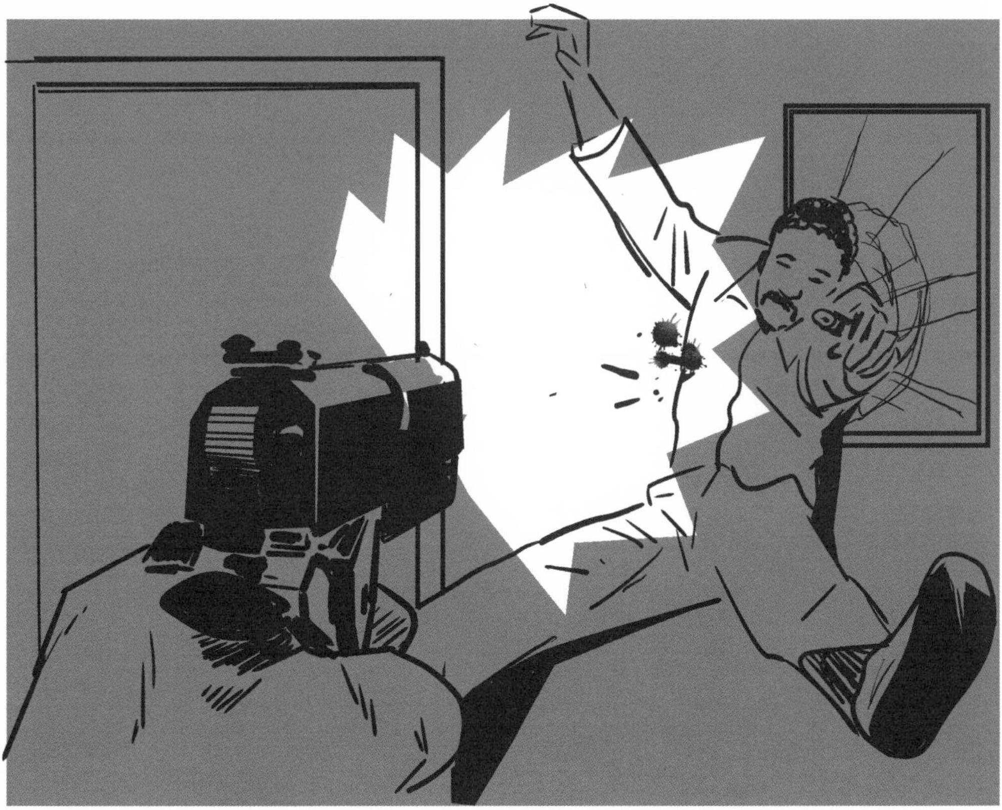

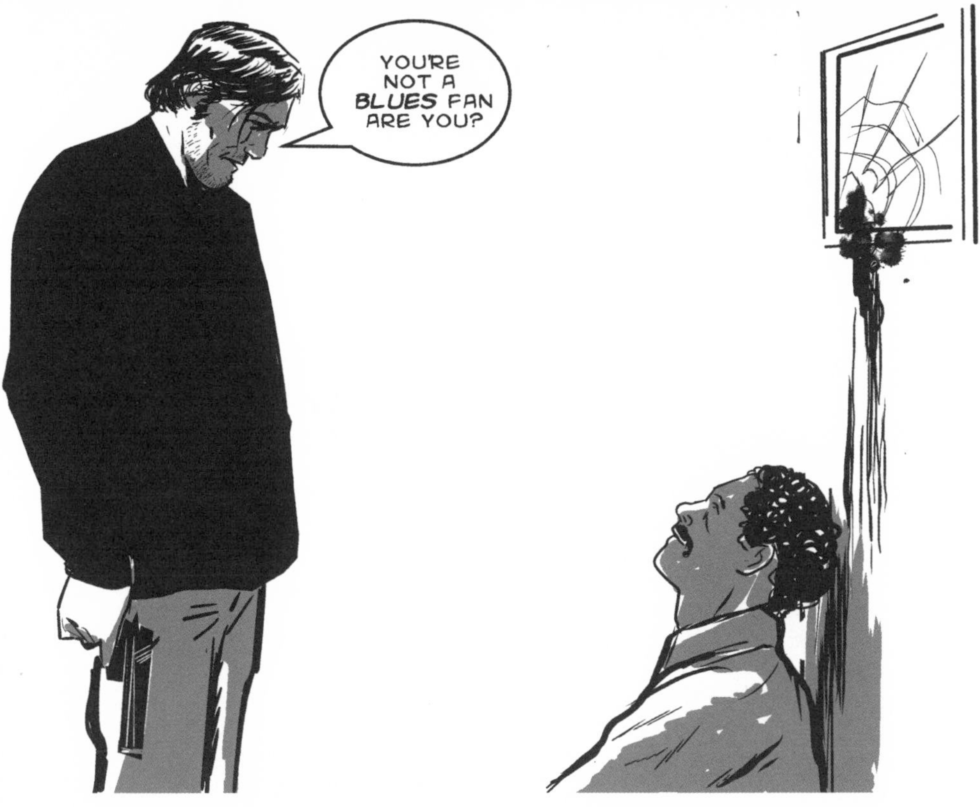
YOU'RE NOT A BLUES FAN ARE YOU?

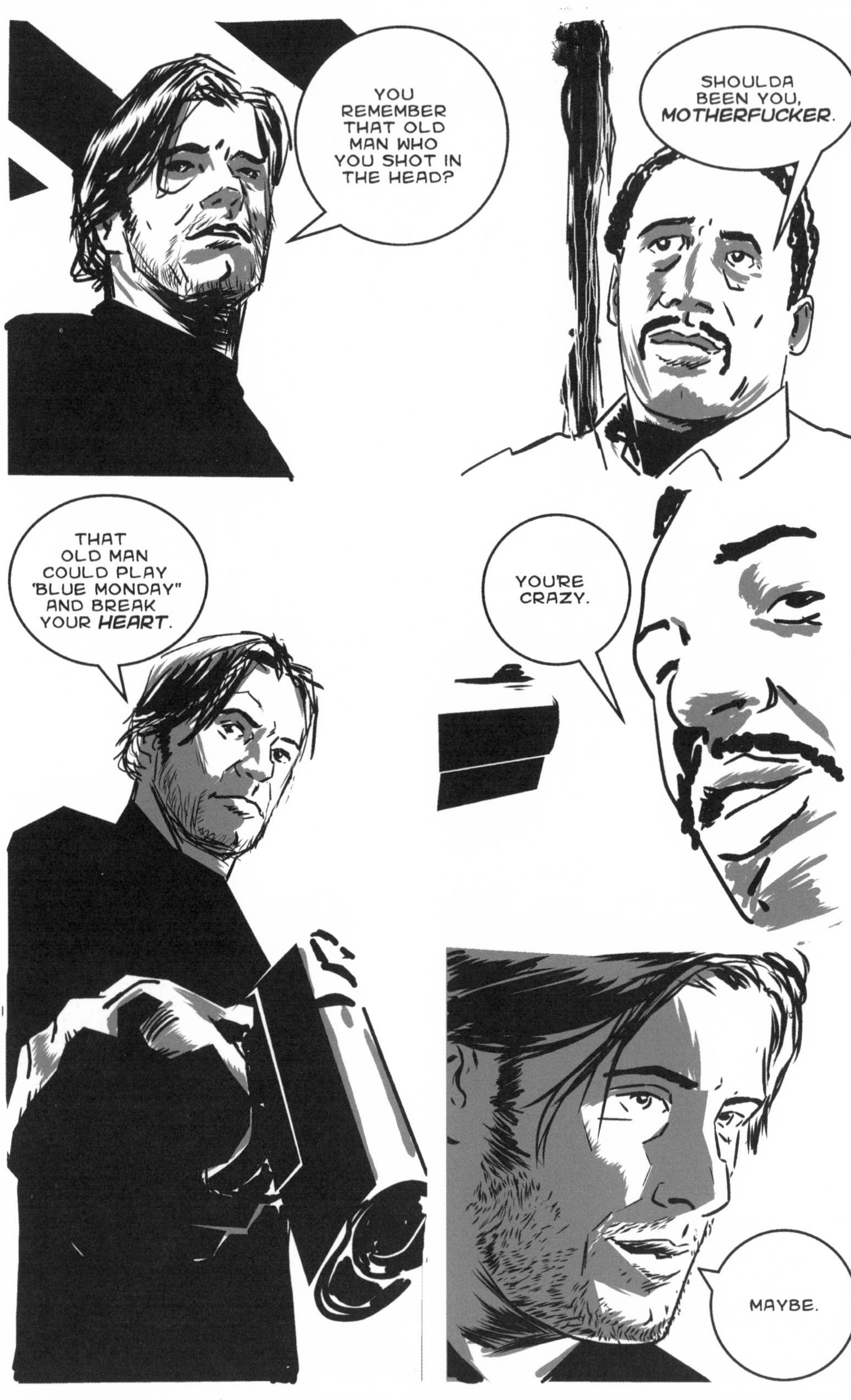
YOU REMEMBER THAT OLD MAN WHO YOU SHOT IN THE HEAD?
SHOULDA BEEN YOU, MOTHERFUCKER.
THAT OLD MAN COULD PLAY "BLUE MONDAY" AND BREAK YOUR HEART.
YOU'RE CRAZY.
MAYBE.

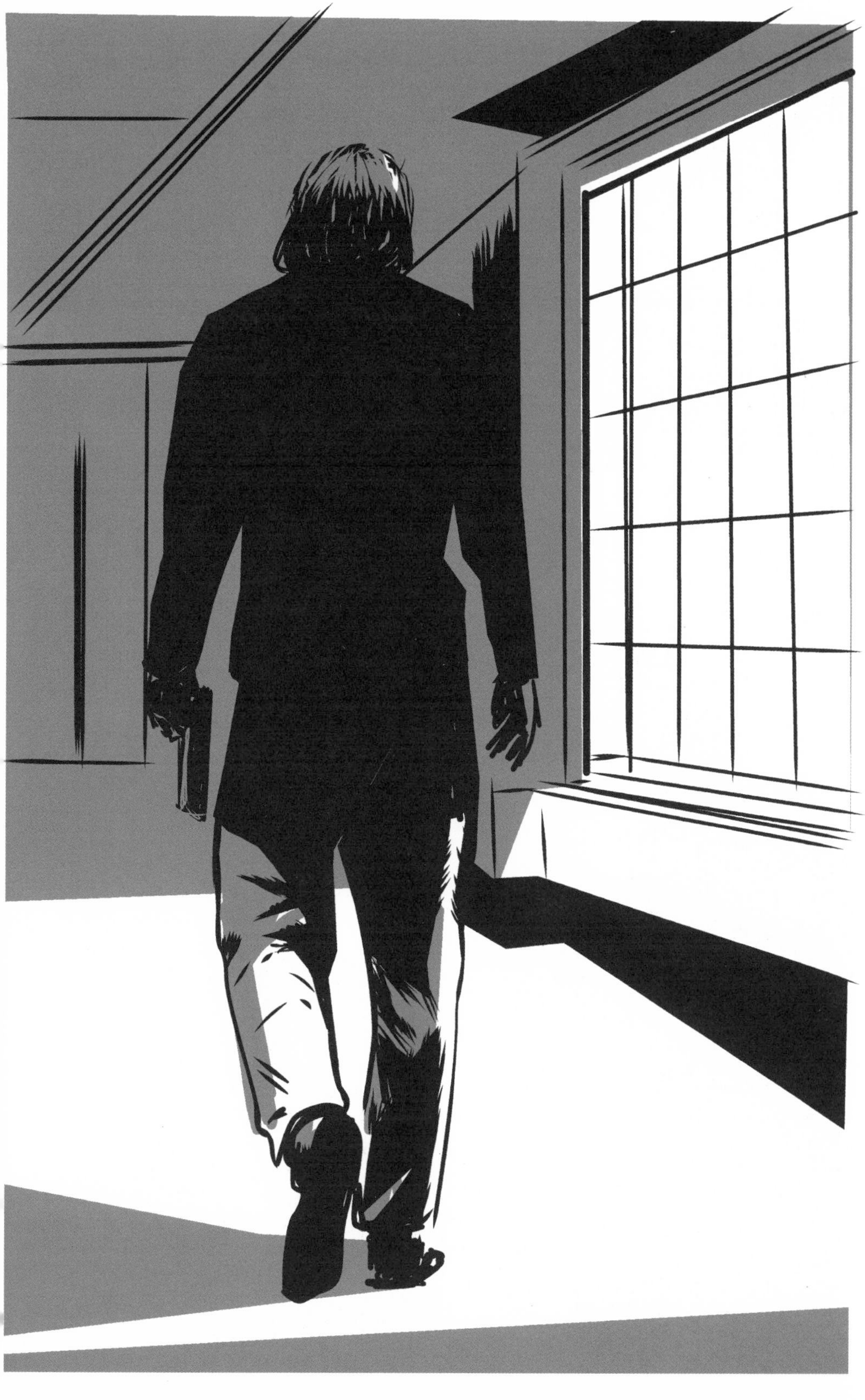

CHAPTER TEN

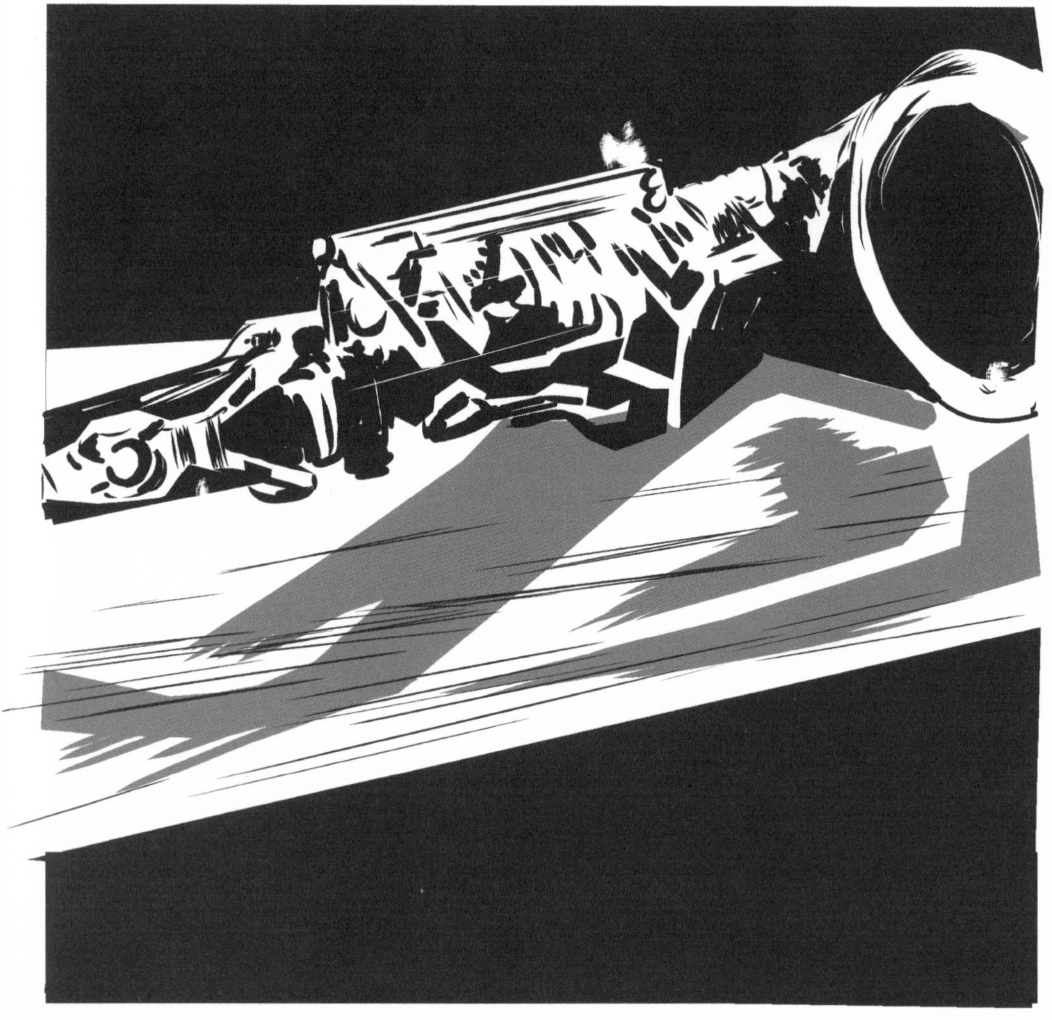

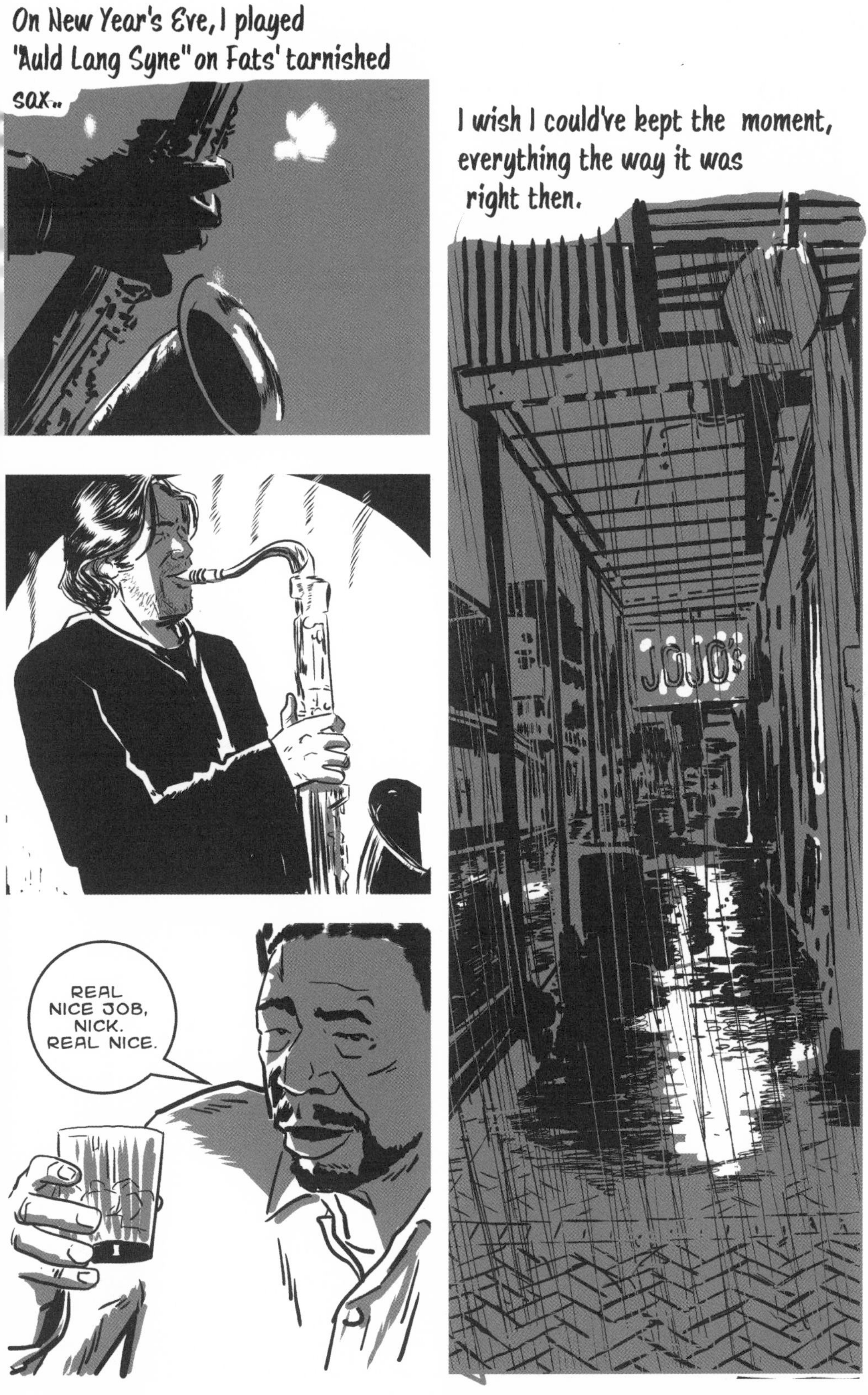
On New Year's Eve, I played "Auld Lang Syne" on Fats' tarnished sax..
REAL NICE JOB, NICK. REAL NICE.
I wish I could've kept the moment, everything the way it was right then.
JOJO's

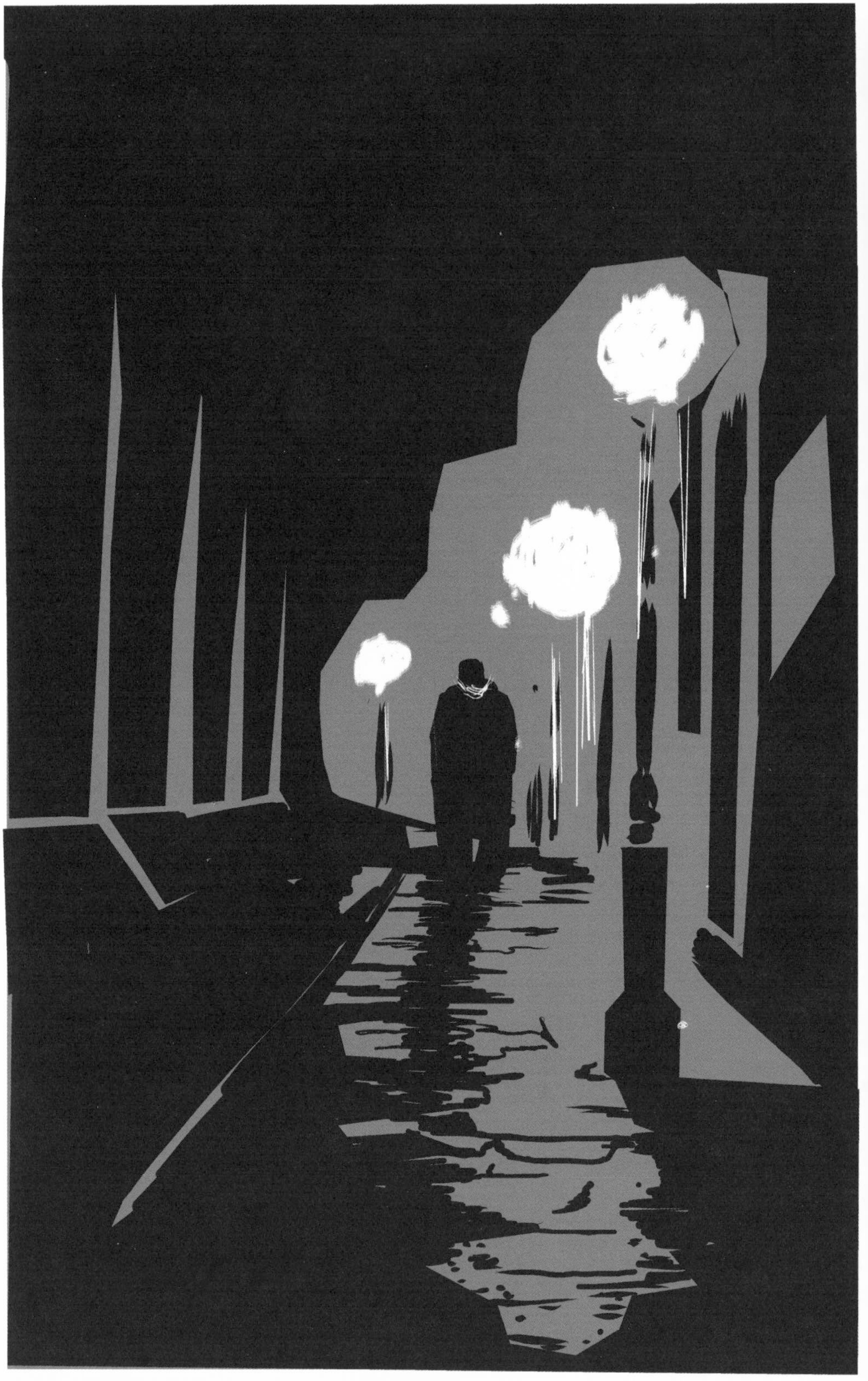

THE BEGINNING...

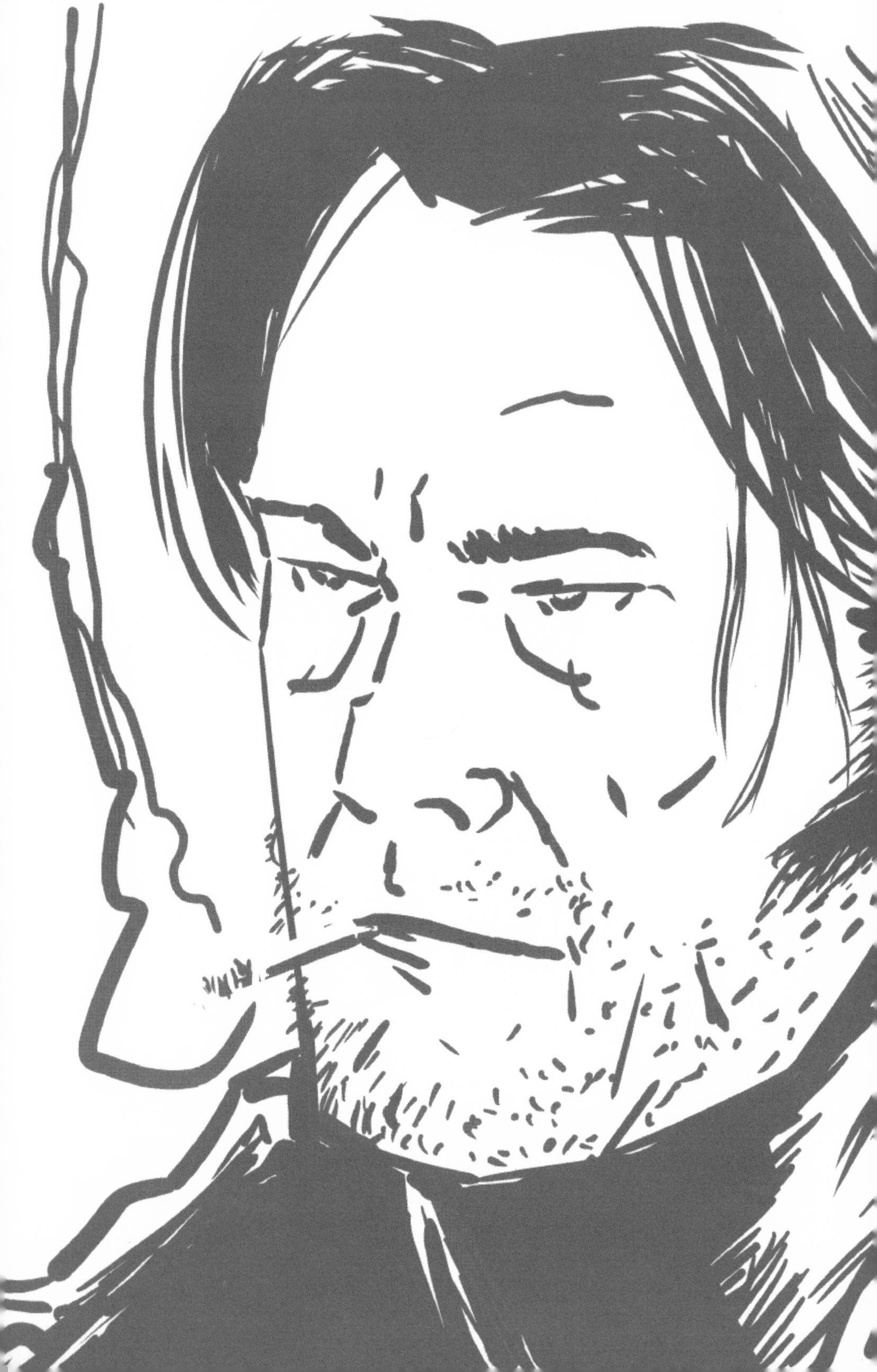

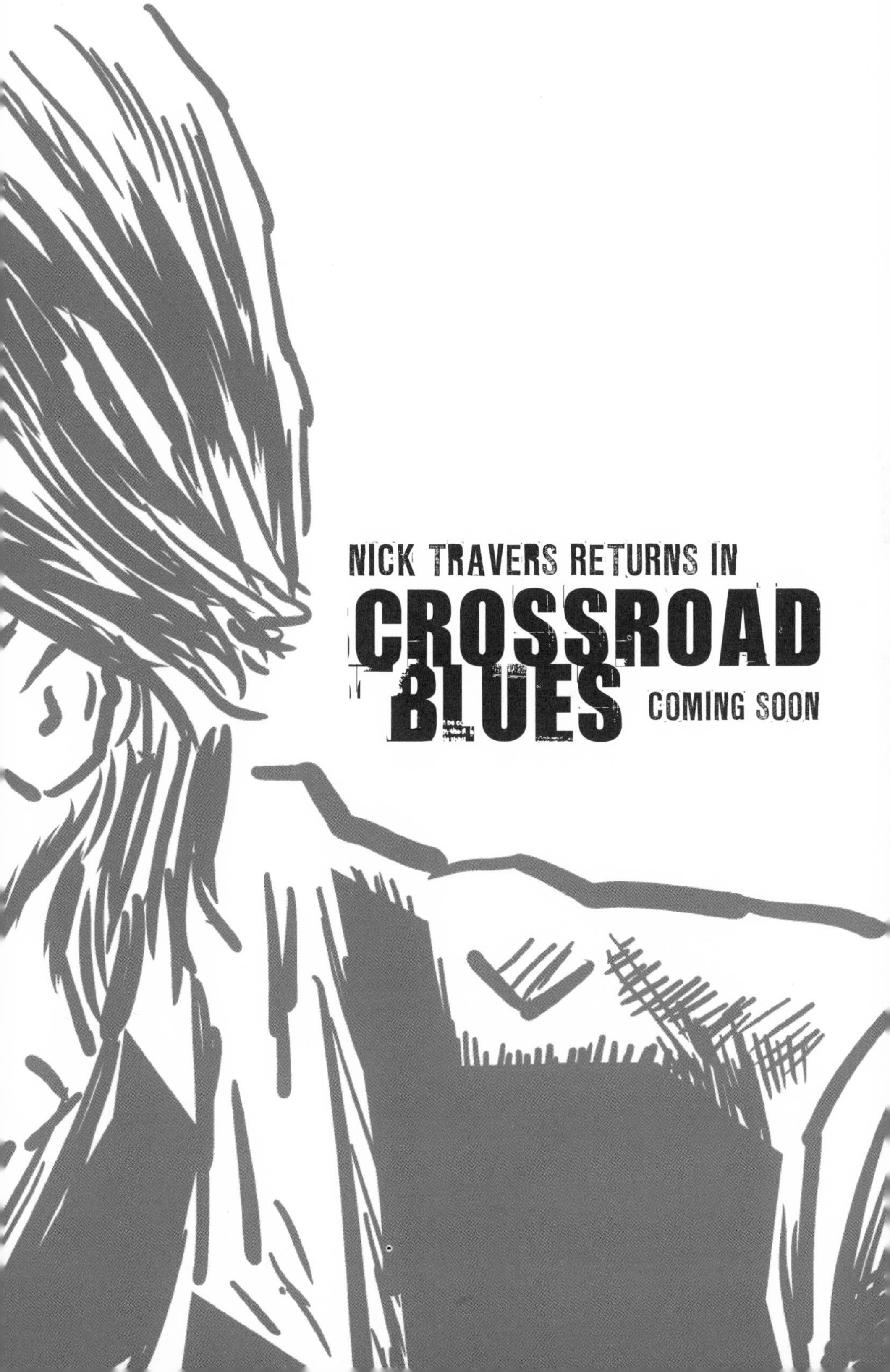
NICK TRAVERS RETURNS IN
CROSSROAD BLUES
COMING SOON

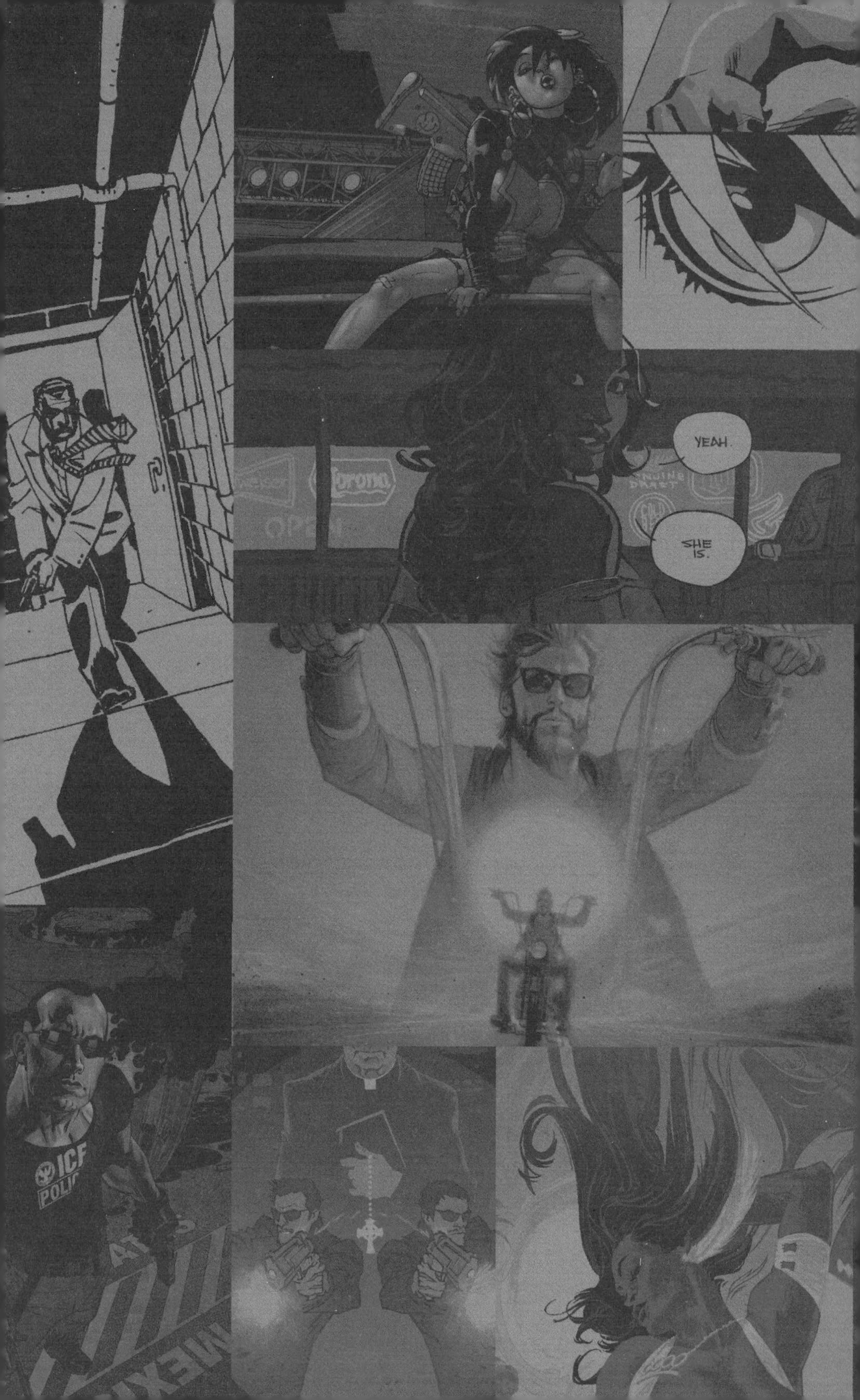
YEAH.
SHE IS.

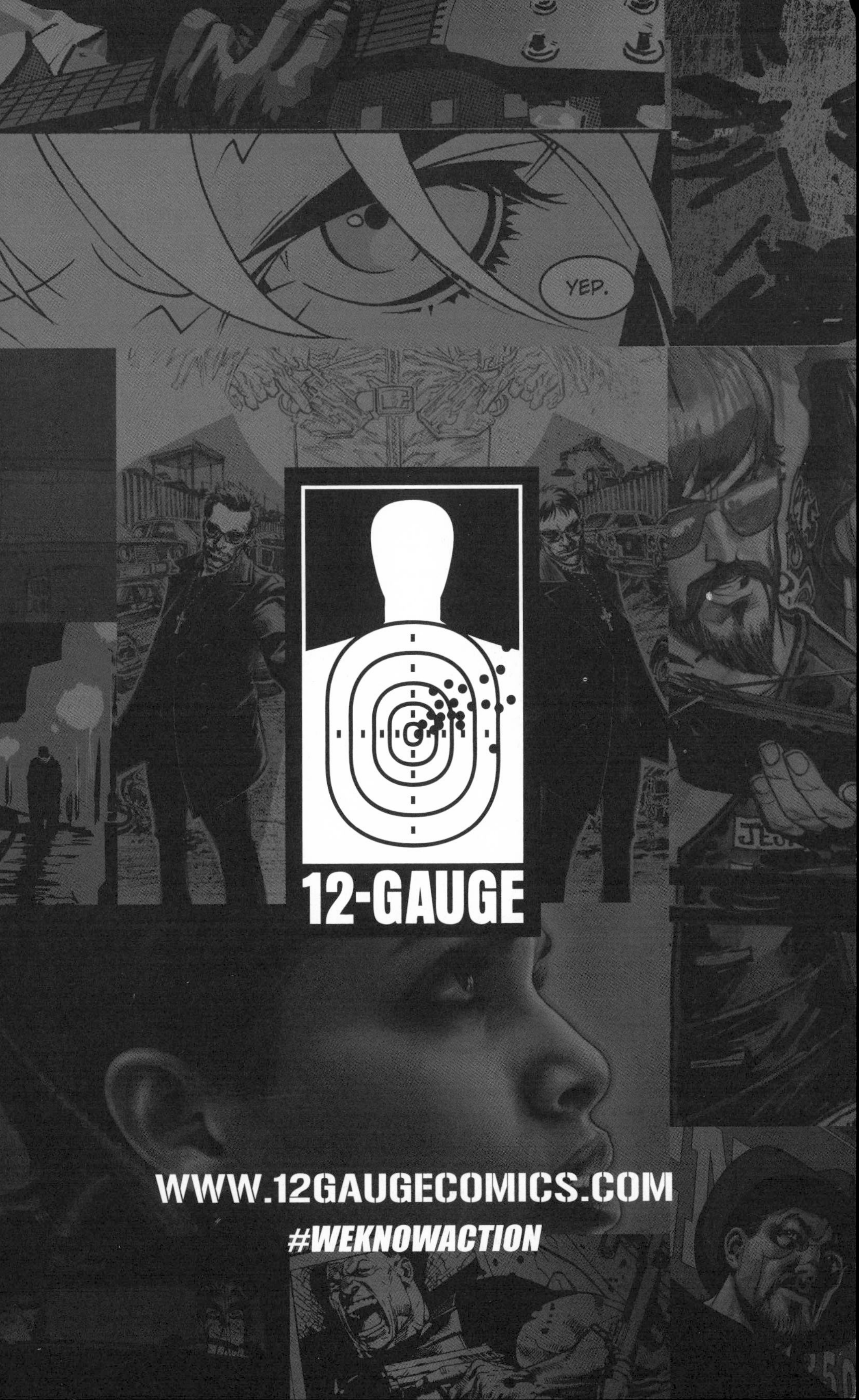
YEP.
12-GAUGE
WWW.12GAUGECOMICS.COM
#WEKNOWACTION

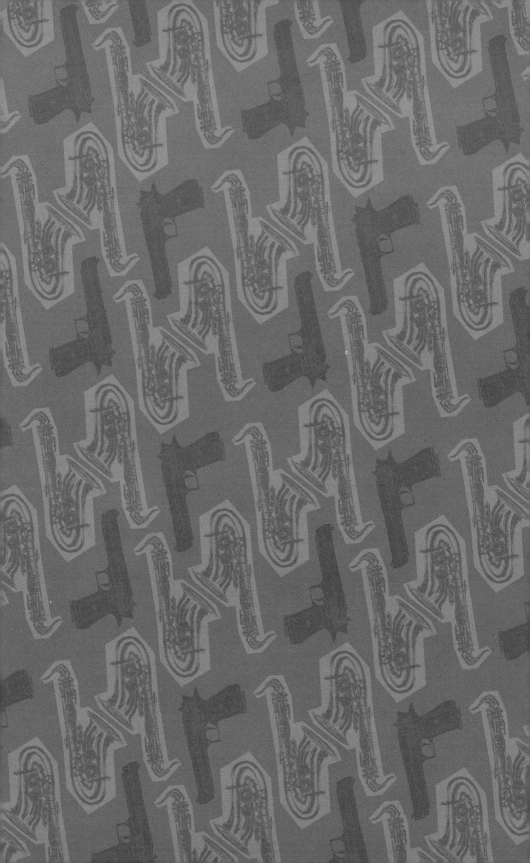